STO

**DO NOT REMOVE
CARDS FROM POCKET**

Sydney, Herself

Colby Rodowsky

Sydney, Herself

Farrar, Straus & Giroux

NEW YORK

Excerpt from "Postscript to Iceland: for W. H. Auden" by
Louis MacNeice is reprinted from *Collected Poems: 1925–1948* by
Louis MacNeice, first published 1949 by Faber and Faber
Limited. Used by permission of the publisher.

To my sons-in-law,
TIL AND JAY

Sydney, Herself

September

It's hard to know just where to begin: with Birdy-Morrison talking about self-awareness, with Sam Klemkoski in the English classroom where he shouldn't have been, or with me and my Boomerang blood.

"Begin at the beginning," my mother always said when I was little and would come running in, telling tales back to front about who did what and to whom.

"Just get it down on paper. We'll mess with it later," said Sam Klemkoski, looking us over that first day of school in September.

Given what I knew about the two of them—that Sam Klemkoski didn't belong there, and that my mother, as mothers go, was generally right—maybe I'd better stick with "Begin at the beginning."

But, first, a warning. This is a school project. Not one of the boring kind, like an outline or a vocabulary drill, but a school project nevertheless. And, of course, to get to the beginning, I had to go back, once I knew it *was* a project, and fill in what already happened.

It was warm for September when my friends Cissy and Mary Jo and I started up the drive to Hawthorne Hills, and the sun, beating down, seemed to make little wavery patches in the air. I felt a trickle of sweat between my shoulder blades, followed by another, and another—a whole river of sweat—and I began to think I should've worn cutoffs and a T-shirt.

"Listen, you guys," I said, urging the other two on, "we didn't spend all summer perfecting our Carol Weatherby look to give up on it now."

"You're right," said Cissy, grinning so that all her teeth, which would have looked big on anybody else but didn't on her, showed.

"I guess," said Mary Jo. Mary Jo's never as sure of things as she ought to be.

We stood staring at one another, and it was as if we were a string of look-alike paper dolls: our hair all permed and cobwebby; our clothes in layers—skirts and shirts and dark-colored stockings, scarves and jackets that reached almost to our knees. ("The three witches from *Macbeth*," my mother called us.) We had a carefully cultivated pallor to our faces, with smudges of eye shadow under our eyes. ("The gray look," my mother called it.) And we walked with our hands sort of out in front as if we were carrying invisible trays. ("As though you're feeling for a doorknob in a dark room," said my mother.)

Carol Weatherby was this really terrific English teacher who taught sophomore creative writing, and all last year and throughout the summer we couldn't wait to be in her class. She's the kind of person who looks misty and tragic, so that you *know* things have happened to her— which definitely haven't to any of us. She told us once last year that she had done her best writing when she was in her early teens and that we, at H.H., were just *ripe* for it. (When I told that to my mother she said, "Sounds like a peach," and went back to her knitting.)

Anyway, there we were, halfway up the school driveway, looking as misty and tragic as we could manage, with everybody around us yelling about summer vacation and how it was good to be back and what kind of kick was Birdy-Morrison going to be on *this* year.

Birdy-Morrison in any other school would've been called the principal (except that any other school probably wouldn't've *hired* her), but at Hawthorne Hills she was "The Head," just as her father, William William Morrison, had been "The Head" (and also founder) before her. And the thing about her was that every summer, when most people were going to the beach or the mountains, she went off to some seminar someplace and came back with a bunch of ideas she tried out on us. And I knew, as we went into the school, that it wouldn't be long before we got this year's offering.

Hawthorne Hills is an alternative and somewhat progressive school where everybody's encouraged to be terrific in at least one thing, which then makes it okay for the same kids to be duds in something else. The main building used to be a private home, but by now it's been added on to so many times and in so many directions that it looks lumpy and slightly run-down. In the middle of the first floor is the Big Hall, which is where we have meetings, plays, concerts, parties, and what pass for assemblies. And which is where we all crowded on that first morning in September to get our "Welcome Back, Girls" talk.

"Welcome back, girls," said Birdy-Morrison when everybody had settled on the floor, the stairs, and into nooks and corners. "Welcome back to Hawthorne Hills." She stood in the center of the room, leaning on the bust of an Indian girl named Mignon and wearing the same dress she'd worn last June when she said "Goodbye, girls." (What I really think is that Birdy-Morrison has six or seven dresses just alike—morning-glory blue with the top permanently sagged out where she sags out—and I imagine her washing them and hanging them on the line the same as I imagine Little Orphan Annie hanging out *her* row of identical dresses.)

"I *know* you all had a wonderful summer—and I *know* you're all glad to be back," chirped Birdy-Morrison. And then there was this rumbly kind of a groan that spread throughout the room—the kind you *know* you're supposed to make when a teacher cracks a joke.

"And that now you're *all* ready to get down to work," she said.

Another groan.

"But first let me share *my* summer with *you*, because this year, girls, I found myself."

"I didn't know she was lost," whispered Cissy, poking me in the ribs.

"I spent part of my vacation at an awareness seminar and I learned to know the inner me," Birdy-Morrison went on. "And that is what I want for you: to know yourselves. Consequently, girls, this year at Hawthorne Hills will be"—significant pause—"the Year of the Self."

By then the heat in the room was beginning to get to me. I tugged at my layers of clothes and wondered if looking like Carol Weatherby was worth it and twisted around to see where she was and if she appreciated my suffering. When I didn't see her, I turned back to Birdy-Morrison, who was going strong.

"Not in a selfish way, girls," she said. "What I want is for you to see yourselves as part of the broad scheme of things. To understand yourselves in light of your relationships, your abilities, the world around you."

"Yuck," said Cissy.

"Maybe next year she'll go to the Grand Canyon," whispered Mary Jo. "Then all we'll have to do is look at slides."

"This year we will have a project," said Birdy-Morrison, her voice quivering. "A yearlong project. And for each of you it will be something different. Those of you who can will express yourselves in the written word . . ." (Here Cissy and Mary Jo and I tilted our chins slightly and tried to look ethereal.)

"Those of you who can draw, who are musical, or gifted in photography will work in those areas . . .

"There will be murals and scrapbooks, plays and oral histories. And so," said Birdy-Morrison, throwing her arms out and setting her bosoms bouncing, "if you can write, write. If you can draw, draw. Whatever your talents, girls, find yourselves."

For a while after that, nobody moved. It reminded me of the time, years ago, when I went to a birthday party at Nancy Parks's and there was a treasure hunt, and after her father gave the instructions, we all waited, the way we were now, until he finally said, "On your mark, get set, *go.*" I halfway expected Birdy-Morrison to say "On your mark, get set, *go.*"

Instead, she said, "There are a few changes you should know about, girls. The parking lot by the back door is for faculty only. There will be a salad bar on Mondays, Wednesdays, and Fridays in the dining room. And Carol Weatherby, who taught creative writing, will not be with

us this year. Her place will be taken by Sam Klemkoski."
And here Birdy-Morrison pointed to a man who was
leaning against the back wall, sort of dozing.

"It's not *fair*," said Cissy as we headed out of the Big
Hall.

"And she didn't even mention it until after the parking
lot and the salad bar on Mondays, Wednesdays, and
Fridays," said Mary Jo.

"And my own mother *knew* it," I said. "She *had* to
know it, the way she was over here all last week for faculty
meetings and stuff."

"Honestly, Sydney," said Cissy. "The only thing that'd
be halfway decent about going to the school where your
mother teaches would be having her *tell* you things. And
yours doesn't."

"Don't remind me," I said. And right away I knew
how really upset Cissy was. Otherwise, she'd never have
mentioned it.

"Carol Weatherby, where are you?" said Mary Jo.

"When we need you most," said Cissy and I together.

But even as we said this, we found ourselves heading
upstairs, through the twisty second-floor hall, to Carol
Weatherby's classroom.

Except that Sam Klemkoski was in it now.

He was not only in it, he was taking up most of it. At
least that's the way it seemed as Cissy and Mary Jo and

I grabbed three desks and shoved them as far over in the corner as we could. But it was hard to get away from Sam Klemkoski. I mean he was so *there*. And right away I knew that, as much as I wanted to look the other way (out of loyalty to Carol), I couldn't take my eyes off him.

Not that he was handsome, or young either. He had this face that looked like it should've had a beard, but didn't; tufts of hair growing out of his ears; a big nose; and a bald spot at the back of his head. His hands were square and sort of beat-up-looking and his clothes were rumpled, the way mine get when I forget and leave them in the dryer for days. And he wore sandals, so his toes showed when he twitched them, which he did every time he said something he thought was important. Or when he was nervous. The way some people do with their eyebrows.

"My name is Sam Klemkoski," he said in a voice that rattled the windowpanes. Twitch-twitch went the toes.

"I'm a wood sculptor" (twitch-twitch) "turned English teacher," he said. "And the reason for the change is that, as an artist, I was afraid I was becoming too isolated, that I was spending too much time staring at my belly button. And I wondered if I could still communicate in words as well as wood. In short, I decided to rejoin the world."

"That means that, whatever happened to Carol, *he* was the only teacher they could get at the last minute," whispered Cissy.

"And I have to confess," Sam Klemkoski went on, "that

the thought of a regular income, no matter how meager, is not entirely unwelcome." (Twitch, twitch, twitch.)

The whole time he was saying this he was balancing a stack of green loose-leaf binders with E.T. on the covers (E.T. in high school?), trying to keep them from slipping and sliding before he handed them out. "Now you all heard Miss Morrison . . ."

"Birdy-Morrison," said Janet Preller from the front of the room.

"Yes," he said. "You heard Miss Morrison tell . . ."

"Birdy-Morrison," said Winkle Shultz from the corner under the hanging spider plant.

"Yes," said Sam, who all of a sudden looked as if he had hold of a greased pig that was just on the point of getting away.

"Hy-phen-ated," said Janet. "Or at least it sounds that way."

"Birdy-Morrison," said Winkle, running the words together. "She goes by her *whole* name, but the teachers just use their first, you know."

Obviously, Sam didn't know, and if he didn't know *that*, then he didn't know much about Hawthorne Hills, which probably made it true what Cissy said about their getting him at the last minute. Like maybe yesterday.

"Well," he said, "that makes me Sam, then. And I'm sure I'll know all your names in the fullness of time."

I watched him handing out those stupid green binders and thought how, since he didn't know anything about

Hawthorne Hills, maybe it was up to the creative-writing class to teach him. Then I yawned and slumped down in my chair, because, with Carol gone, I felt sad and sort of blah and not up to teacher baiting (which takes more energy than one might imagine).

"Now," said Sam, wiping his hands down the sides of his pants, "you all heard Miss . . . you all heard Birdy-Morrison talking about self-awareness. You have all been given these notebooks, and I want you to cleave unto them; to make them your own, your boon companions."

Cleave? Boon companions? Fullness of time? I wrote on the first page of my notebook and shoved it over for Cissy to see.

"Good," said Sam Klemkoski, bringing his hand down flat on the top of a bookcase so that dust puffed out from the shelves. "I'm glad to see that some of you are already taking notes, because that's what this year will be all about. A series of notes. One long observation that will be made up of stories and character sketches, essays and scraps of dialogue. This year will be a little bit of everything: a hodgepodge, a gallimaufry. You will find your own voice. But, always, in what context?"

"Self-awareness," said Winkle Schultz, but her *voice* said, "This is only the first day of school and I'm already bored."

"Yes, self-awareness," said Sam. And then after a humongous pause, when you could almost see him figuring out in his mind that class wasn't over yet and he'd better say something, he asked, "And how do you plan to carry out Birdy-Morrison's project this year?"

"We can express our innermost feelings," I said mistily.

"And explore the fathoms of our minds," said Mary Jo, in a voice that was hardly more than a whisper.

"And wait for inspiration," added Cissy.

"No!" roared Sam. "This is a writing class, not Melodrama 101. If you want to have the vapors, go to the infirmary. In this class I want good writing, good nouns, good strong action words. And be forewarned, I didn't live lo these many years to have it all end in a morass of adjectives."

There was a whimpering sound, and I closed my eyes and imagined the ghost of Carol Weatherby slinking over the windowsill and down the rainspout. When I looked again, the room seemed sharper and had a decidedly masculine smell—like wood chips and burned toast. And once again I felt bereft.

"You will write about what's going on in your lives," said Sam.

(Fine. Swell. There's nothing going on in my life. Absolutely nothing.)

"You will write about your parents."

(I live with my mother, who is so positively normal she's a weirdo by default.)

"And now," he said, "you will write about your summer vacation. Just get it down on paper. We'll mess with it later."

"Yuck," said Mary Jo.

"I don't believe this," said Cissy.

"The way we'll work it in this class is that you'll keep a day-to-day journal," said Sam. "Then you'll put all special assignments on fresh pieces of paper, though from time to time I'll ask to see the whole binder. This should not, in any way, inhibit you. Nothing you write will be held against you, no matter how honest."

"How about private? I mean, some things are private," said Mary Jo, and I thought for a minute she was going to cry.

Sam must've thought so, too, because he sort of slipped into his greased-pig look again and said, "If any of you has anything that you consider absolutely private, fasten those pages with a paper clip, or simply remove them. And I will respect that privacy. Trust me."

Trust me. Trust me? I opened my notebook, picked up my pen, and then sat chewing on the end of it and thinking how yesterday, even though it was the last day of vacation, life was okay. And how suddenly today it was really the pits: with Carol Weatherby gone and my clothes creeping up around me all hot and itchy and now somebody named Sam Klemkoski telling me to trust him and to write about my summer vacation (which I couldn't do even if I wanted to because it was a basic bore).

I wrote *My Summer Vacation* across the top of the paper, then bit down hard on the end of my pen, rolling the plastic back and forth between my teeth. A horsefly buzzed against the screen and from the hockey field came the sound of a power mower. My mind felt flat and spongy and my hand was heavy as I started to write.

My Summer Vacation

It's hard to use good strong action words to describe my summer vacation because basically there wasn't any (good strong action). My summer was dull.

About the only thing that happened was that Cissy and Mary Jo and I hung out at the mall some (except that I think that's a really dumb place to hang out).

The only other thing that happened was that I met Porter Martin, this neat little kid who moved into the house in back of mine. The way I met him was that one day I was outside sitting in the sun when I heard a "screech-thlunk" kind of a sound. "Screech-thlunk, screech-thlunk, screech-thlunk." I finally got up and went through the bushes and into the next yard, where there was an enormous trampoline with this little kid bouncing on it. ("Screech-thlunk.") Right away he beckoned and moved over to make room for me (which was sort of wild because I'd never been on a trampoline before), and for a while we just bounced and talked (as much as you can talk on a trampoline). The thing about Porter is that he talks funny. I mean, no matter what anyone says he repeats it with an "sm" in front of it. Like I said, "I'm Sydney," and he said, "Sydney Smydney."

It takes a while to have a conversation that way, but I did find out that he had just moved here from Connecticut and that he had an older brother who went to boarding school in the winter and to camp in the summer.

Another thing. After we'd been bouncing awhile, Porter's mother came out and asked me if I baby-sat, and if I did, would I like to watch Porter some this summer. Which worked out well, because Porter's an okay kid and I'm an okay baby-sitter—but it's my personal opinion that Mrs. Martin would've hired King Kong if he'd happened to have been jumping up and down on the trampoline that day.

And that basically sums up my summer. A bummer. Smummer.

I was just sitting there, staring at what I had written, when Sam swooped down and picked up my paper. He took it over to the window and stood reading it, pulling on his chin and nodding from time to time.

"Not bad," he said after a while. "But I'd like to see you extend it, and work on the *sounds* of boredom—if in fact you *were* bored. There are some character sketches just waiting to be written here, and I particularly like the use of '*screech-thlunk.*' But watch out for those parentheses."

And right away I felt as if somebody'd cut off my feet

and told me to walk. (Anyway, who did he think he was, taking away my parentheses?)

But, before I could say anything, he was handing that paper back to me and saying, "Your name is?"

"Sydney."

"Sydney who?"

"Sydney Downie."

And Sam was across the room, writing SYDNEY DOWNIE DOWN DOWN? on the blackboard in big splotchy capital letters and acting like he was some kind of genius. As if nobody'd ever thought of that before.

"Yeah," I said. "My father was a Boomerang."

"Which one? Clive, Oscar, Jamie, or Pudge?" he asked.

"I'm not sure," I said, suddenly furious with him for thinking he was so cool (which he's not), and for being there in the first place.

And all the while Sam was standing there saying, "Sydney Downie . . . Sydney Downie . . . Sydney Downie Down Down . . ." as if it were this terrific-sounding phrase, and I remembered the time some teacher in elementary school had told us that "cellar door" was the most pleasing sound in the English language.

"Sydney Downie . . . cellar door . . ." I said to myself as I got up to go. There are no bells at Hawthorne Hills, everybody just keeps track of the time. Everybody except Sam Klemkoski, that is. I mean, there we all were halfway down the hall with him coming after us calling, "Remember, girls. Work on your journals. Extend your summer pieces. And, Sydney, search for the sounds of boredom."

"Did you know that I have Boomerang blood in my veins?" I said to Porter Martin when we were sitting on his back steps later that afternoon.

"Boomer blood, Smoomer blood," said Porter.

"What do *you* know?" I said, getting up and going through the hedge to my own house. (It wasn't until after I'd put that down in my journal that I realized I'd written what Sam would call a scrap of dialogue.) I took an apple from one of our shelves in Mrs. Hubbard's refrigerator, waited awhile, and went back out. I mean, it wasn't Porter's fault that I'd had a rotten day.

"And you know what else?" he said, as if I'd been there all along.

"No, what?"

"My brother Wally's got about a million Boomerang records and posters in his room on the third floor and I'd take you up and show you, only my mother has company and she said for me to not come in."

What I wanted to say was how come, if this Wally brother was such a Boomerang freak, he'd gone off to school and not taken his records with him. But I didn't because by then I was angry—with Porter's mother for not even allowing her own kid inside just because she had company, and with Porter for not caring. The way I see it, people should care intensely about things.

"How come?" said Porter, getting up and going over to the trampoline.

"How come what?"

"How come you have Boomer blood?"

"Because my father was a Boomerang."

"How do you know?"

"Because of my name—Sydney Downie—and it being sort of the same as one of their albums, *Sydney Downie Down Down.*"

"That's neat," said Porter, jumping high and landing flat on his back.

"Yeah," I said.

"Neat smeat," said Porter.

After supper I went back and filled in my journal from the very first moment of school this morning. And by the time I was ready to take my bath I realized two things. One was that if I kept it up at the rate I was going, I'd have something the size of *Gone with the Wind* by Christmas, and the other was that maybe I did have Boomerang blood in my veins.

I mean, why not?

I mean, I had to have somebody's, didn't I?

Somebody other than just a high school history teacher. I mean, it takes two, doesn't it?

I settled down in the bathtub and thought how all of

a sudden I didn't believe the story my mother'd always told me. Oh, parts of it were okay, I guess. I'm sure that when her father died he *did* leave my mother enough money to go to Australia for a year of graduate study at the University of Sydney, and that she *did* go, and that it probably *was* the best year of her life. But then it gets fuzzy: that whole thing about her meeting a student named Arthur Downie in a secondhand bookstore and how they fell in love and got married; how just a month before I was born he was killed in a car accident, and when I was three weeks old she brought me back to the States, because it was *home*. Mom even says she named me Sydney because that's where she and my father met. The whole thing is sad, and romantic—but fuzzy.

Like the reason she gives for why there is just that one crinkled snapshot of Arthur Downie (and his face so shadowy that he could be *anybody*)—that she'd lost her really good one and never ever been able to find it.

I slid down lower in the tub and thought about my mother and the Boomerangs, and that was a really weird idea. My *mother* and the *Boomerangs*.

Talk about mind-boggling. I mean, the Boomerangs were so awesome, just like the Beatles and the Who and the Grateful Dead.

But, anyway, which Boomer? And right away I decided it wasn't Clive because I couldn't bear to have what happened to Clive happen to *my* father. I mean, the way he just *disappeared* and no one knew what became of him.

Oscar? Jamie? Or Pudge? I knew that would take some investigating, and then I saw how finding out who I was would fit right in with Birdy-Morrison's self-awareness project: me in the broad scheme of things.

And then another thought poked at me. How come my mother and the Boomerang split up? It probably had something to do with Mom not knowing anything about music (it's embarrassing, but whenever we go shopping together and I drag her into the Jumpin' Jeans and you can hardly *hear* the stereo, she says things like "Why don't they turn that noise *off?*"). Either that, or the way she goes to bed in a flannel nightgown and socks all winter long. I mean, it's obvious she never read any of those articles they're always running in *Cosmo*, like "101 Ways to Keep Your Marriage Alive."

The way I see it, she could have made an effort. At least for my sake.

Then Mom was on the other side of the door, knocking and telling me to hurry so she could take a bath, and reminding me that Mrs. Hubbard, our landlady, who pretends—when it suits her—not to be, hated for us to run the water late at night. (Now, Mrs. Hubbard's another story. I'll get to her.)

It was obvious by about the second week of school that Sam Klemkoski had had a crash course in teaching. And he had his toes under better control, too. I mean, by then we had revised our summer-vacation pieces about a dozen times and had dog-eared the dictionary. As far as anybody could tell, he wasn't so much interested in the depths of our feelings as in whether we could spell.

Sam may have been more comfortable in the classroom, but the topics he gave us to write about were still pretty gross. "My School, to Someone Who Doesn't Know Anything about It," in four strong sentences or less. Now, *come* on.

My School, to Someone Who Doesn't Know Anything about It

At Hawthorne Hills there is an underlying faith in the goodness of the child. There is a strong emphasis on freedom of expression, and it is considered healthy to say what you think. As schools go, I guess it's not too bad.

Note from Sam Klemkoski to Sydney Downie: *I could have learned as much from the catalogue.*

It was pretty obvious from this that he'd been the "Someone Who Doesn't Know Anything about It" and was just trying to pump us, but at least he had the decency not to make us revise this time around. (Well, you can't get blood from a turnip, as Mrs. Hubbard sometimes says.) Anyway, we'd no sooner recovered from that than he threw us another real winner.

I'm embarrassed to mention it, but here goes.

*   *   *

Note from Sydney Downie to Sam Klemkoski: *About that last sentence—you* said *we could be totally honest.*

A Description of My Mother

Probably right at this moment everybody in class is sitting here trying to remember exactly what her mother looks like (the way sometimes late at night or in the middle of geometry you close your eyes and try to see *a person you know really well, only you can't, and that sort of freaks you out). I don't have that problem. The reason is that my mother just walked past the door, and as soon as she gets a cup of coffee she'll walk past going the other way. That's part of a problem I do have. Or maybe that* is *the problem.*

Sometimes, going to school where my mother teaches can be a real drag. Sometimes, it makes my skin crawl to hear other kids groaning about a paper that's due or a book they have to read, and know that it's all her doing. Kids pretty much like her, though—or they don't not *like her—but it'd be hard to imagine any of them wanting to look like her, or even* be *like her.*

My mother has many fine qualities, but she is definitely not cool. She is, in fact, sort of like oatmeal and plain brown wrapping paper, like white sheets and bars of sturdy Ivory soap in the bathroom. She is kind to animals and always drops money in the top hat of any street musician we happen to pass.

Her name is Martha (after Martha Washington), which

may explain why she grew up to be a history teacher. (I can't help wondering what you grow up to be if you're named after a city.)

Note from Sam Klemkoski to Sydney Downie: *You did not do the assignment as asked. This is hardly a description of your mother, though it tells me a lot about you. There is merit in the third-from-the-last sentence but, on the whole, I'd like you to rewrite the piece.*

Revision

A Description of My Mother

One might think, looking at my mother, that she is like oatmeal and plain brown wrapping paper; that she is like white sheets and bars of Ivory soap in the bathroom. One might think she teaches at Hawthorne Hills because of the security (and the free tuition) and so she'll have a family of sorts (even if it is Birdy-Morrison and the others). And that she never does anything really exciting.

But that's not true. Because my mother was once married to one of the Boomerangs and, apparently, in the heyday of her youth she was filled with passion. I like to imagine her sitting through rehearsals and recording sessions, and when I listen to the records I'm <u>sure</u> that some of the songs were written for her. Probably something from "Sydney Downie Down Down" because of her naming me for that particular album.

Well, at least she left off the last two "Downs."

Note from Sydney Downie to Sam Klemkoski: *My mother's a very private person, so <u>please</u> don't mention this to her.*

Notes from Sam Klemkoski to Sydney Downie: *(1) Heydays and youth don't necessarily go hand in hand. (2) Mum's the word.*

October

"Oscar Meeks.

"Jamie Ward.

"Pudge.

"And Sydney who?" I said out loud. Then I pushed aside the Boomerang books that were spread out on the bed around me and listened to the rain beating on the windowpane and thought how, just since this afternoon, October had turned into fall. The house seemed empty, and kind of rattly. My mother was over at school for a meeting, and even though Mrs. Hubbard was downstairs, sometimes Mrs. Hubbard *there* was the same as Mrs. Hubbard *not there*.

I reached for the phone and called Cissy, but her line

was busy. Then I called Mary Jo and *her* line was busy, so I knew they were talking to each other and that as soon as they hung up one of them would call me and then afterward I'd call the other one. I balanced the phone on my stomach, thinking that my mother let me have a phone of my own as a concession to our not having an apartment of our own. I closed my eyes and could almost hear her saying, "But you were *with* those girls all day in school." (My mother is *so* predictable.)

I picked up the paper and read Ann Landers, about how half the people in the world think toilet paper should go on the roller one way (over the top) and the other half think it should go another (out from under). I began my geometry homework and decided it made as much sense as the Great Toilet Paper Debate, so I put it away. I opened my history book, then remembered that I had two free periods before class tomorrow and, instead, fished around in my journal until I found Sam's creative-writing assignment. But once I'd found it I just sat staring at it.

Then I heard Mrs. Hubbard downstairs, shaking the cat-food box and calling Dimples, and right away it was as if a thousand light bulbs went off inside my head. Even though Sam spends half his time reminding us that Edison described genius as "one percent inspiration and ninety-nine percent perspiration," I was pretty sure I'd had not only an inspiration—but an inspiration of genius.

Just then the phone rang and I picked it up, saying, "I've had an inspiration."

"Sam says that Edison said . . ." Cissy began.

"I know all that," I said. "But look at tomorrow's assignment. Read it to me."

And there was a rustling noise before I heard her recite, in a singsong voice, " 'There are peripheral people in our lives. Tell about one of them.' "

"Mis-sis Hub-bard," I said.

"You've had an inspiration," said Cissy.

"Yeah," I said, smiling and licking my lips.

When I hung up after talking to Cissy, I called Mary Jo and said, "I need an opening sentence about Mrs. Hubbard for Sam's assignment."

"Weird," said Mary Jo.

"Weird?"

"Yeah, as in 'My landlady, Mrs. Hubbard, is weird.' "

"Too general," I said. "Can't you just see Sam twiddling his toes and saying, 'Too general'? Anyway, she's not exactly our landlady. At least she pretends not to be."

"That's what makes her weird," said Mary Jo. "That, and the cats."

"And the birds," I said, writing *Mrs. Hubbard—cats— birds—weird* on a scrap of paper and hoping it would mush itself into something.

It didn't, though, and by the time I hung up, all I still had was *Mrs. Hubbard—cats—birds—weird*. I reached for the thesaurus, looked up *weird* and found about a million subheadings: *awesome, creepy, deathly, eerie, foolish, odd, sorcerous.* "None of the above," I said to myself. "Except maybe *odd.*" So I wrote *odd* on my paper and went downstairs to get a Coke.

When I got to the kitchen, the cat, Dimples, was asleep on the stove and I stopped for a minute to rub behind her ears. The funny thing was that, as I stood there rubbing, a sentence started taking shape in my head. "It's not that Mrs. Hubbard has had so many cats . . ." I thought as I grabbed my Coke and headed back upstairs, whispering the words to myself to keep from forgetting them.

Mrs. Hubbard

It's not that Mrs. Hubbard has had so many cats, but that they're all named Dimples. One at a time, one after the other, with no break in between. What she really wants you to think is that there's been only one cat all along—from the first one she ever owned until now. (And sometimes the <u>new</u> Dimples doesn't look anything like the <u>old</u> Dimples.)

My mother told me that when we first moved here (I was too young to remember) Dimples was a black cat with three white feet. One day Mom and I came home from work (can you believe I used to spend all day in a playpen at Hawthorne Hills?) and there was a ginger cat on the kitchen windowsill. "Oh, I see you have a new cat," my mother said. And Mrs. Hubbard looked her straight in the eye and said, "I can't imagine _what_ you're talking about. Surely you recognize Dimples."

I have only my mother's word for that first incident (though she's generally reliable—except for the matter of my Boomerang blood), but I was practically an eyewitness to the next _cat_astrophe. It happened just this past August.

I'd been at the mall with Cissy and Mary Jo (it was the day we got our hair permed), and when I got home, there was a tall skinny tortoiseshell cat swinging from the curtain in the kitchen. Mrs. Hubbard was there, shaking the box of cat food. It was sort of like one of those creepy experiences when something happens and all of a sudden you're sure it's happened before. I said, "Hey, a new cat." And she said, "Nonsense. You've known Dimples all your life."

When I heard the "screech-thlunk" of the trampoline, I went looking for Porter, grumbling about the new cat that was supposedly an old cat. Then he told me how the real Dimples ran out in front of a florist's truck, and how afterward Mrs. Hubbard and the driver (both crying) wrapped the cat in burlap and buried it alongside the garage. Porter watched this through the hedge, and later, when he was going around the block on his pogo stick, he saw Mrs. Hubbard getting out of her car with a cat carrier that was lurching from side to side.

I was upstairs, hanging over the railing, when I heard my mother come in that day. "Oh, a new . . ." I heard

her say. And then, "Well, hello, Dimples. How are you?"
(Never say my mother doesn't learn from her mistakes.)

I looked over what I'd written and thought that it was okay but not terrific and that maybe tonight I just wasn't up to ninety-nine percent perspiration. I guess I should've put in the part that even though *we* supposedly didn't notice the new Dimples the *birds* certainly did. The birds belong to Mrs. Hubbard and she keeps them in cages on the sun porch, except when she lets them all fly loose every morning while she watches the *Today* show. Well, what happened was that the day after the tortie Dimples arrived I woke up to this horrendous scream, went running downstairs, and stood frozen there on the outside of the glass door, watching Mrs. Hubbard chasing Dimples chasing birds. (Later that afternoon there was a bird-sized grave next to the cat-sized grave, which of course we all just kept pretending wasn't there at all.)

Anyway, I put "Mrs. Hubbard" away, reached for the largest Boomerang book, and turned to the picture of their album *The Boomerangs' G'day.* Then I took it into the bathroom, propping it up on the clothes hamper, examining their faces. And my own in the mirror.

I ran my finger over Pudge's receding hairline and thought how I couldn't be related to someone who didn't use any name other than "Pudge."

I studied Oscar's face and decided that, even at fifteen,

I looked more sophisticated than he did. (Is that kind of thing hereditary?)

I stared at Jamie, comparing his eyes to mine. We had the same streaky brown hair, and I pulled mine back so it looked short on the sides, letting it hang down in back and wondering how I'd look with spiky bangs.

I tried not to see Clive Miller because of the way it made me feel sad and as if I knew the ending of a movie before it began.

I looked back at Pudge, at Oscar, at Jamie, and then leaned in closer to the mirror, so that my breath steamed the glass.

"Sydney, what on earth are you doing?" said my mother, appearing suddenly in the doorway.

"Looking for zits," I said, jumping away and rubbing my face and nudging the hamper with my foot all at the same time. I heard the book slide down against the wall.

Note from Sam Klemkoski to Sydney Downie: *Your paper on Mrs. Hubbard works on some level because I want to know more. Is she a relative? Please extend this by Monday, then we'll see about putting it all together. F.Y.I.—that creepy feeling is called déjà vu. And watch those sentence fragments.*

Watch them do what? I wanted to write back, but when I reread Sam's note—the part about Mrs. Hubbard and me being related—what I really wanted to do was throw up. I was sitting in the library and all of a sudden I felt mad and kind of grossed out, like Lucy in *Peanuts* when Snoopy comes near her and she yells, "Dog germs!" I wrote DOG GERMS across the bottom of my paper, then rubbed my hands across the tabletop until they squeaked.

"Is anything wrong, Sydney?" said Maddie Stephens, the librarian, leaning across the desk and looking at me.

"Just getting rid of dog germs," I said. And when she kept standing there, waiting, the way librarians sometimes do, I added, "I have to find out something about Australia."

"What kind of something?"

"It's for creative writing. Sam told us to start taking notes for a piece called 'I Would Like to Go to—— Because——' and where I want to go is Australia."

"Me, too," said Maddie Stephens, sighing and getting a wistful look in her eyes. "I've been saving to go there. Come over here and I'll show you where the travel books are."

As I followed her to the far end of the library, she asked, "Any place in particular you had in mind?"

"Sydney," I said, "because of my mother going to *school* there. And because of my father being *born* there."

"I didn't know your father was an Aussie," said Maddie. "I thought maybe it was because of your name, or that you were a Boomerang fan."

"I *am* a fan, and a daughter, too. One of the Boomerangs is my father."

"And Clark Gable was mine, at least that's what I used to pretend," she said, laughing and pulling books off the shelf. "Except that I had red hair and freckles just like my mother's husband, so it was hard not to acknowledge him. Which Boomerang, by the way?"

"I'm not sure," I said.

"Pudge was always my favorite," she said.

"I'm narrowing it down."

"There was something about him."

"Between Oscar and Jamie," I said.

"Well, yes," she said. "Anyway, here are the books."

I went back to my table and thumbed through the books Maddie had shown me. Then I shoved them aside and pulled a Boomerang book out of my knapsack, opening to the first chapter. I'd always heard from Mom that Sydney (the city) was great, and I had to admit it looked okay. Exciting, but sort of comfortable. I turned to the pictures of the houses the Boomerangs had lived in when they were little and they were all pretty much the same, except that Pudge's was the largest and Clive's the smallest and there was a flower garden in front of Oscar's. Jamie's house was brick, with a tile roof and lace curtains at the windows and a wooden door with a brass knocker. I found a paragraph that told about Jamie's father being a butcher and his mother a schoolteacher, and how they both used to go hear the Boomerangs play when they were just starting out and not at all famous. And afterward his mother'd take everybody back home and fix them steak and eggs. I thought how even though the house was small, at least it was theirs and not shared with somebody like Mrs. Hubbard. I scratched at the picture as if I half expected the curtains to open so I could see inside, but just then the fire alarm rang and I had to drop everything and go outside. (If there's one thing Hawthorne Hills is *not* casual about, it's fire drills.) And when we came in, there was just time to grab my books and get to math.

All of a sudden, October was half over, and what with homework and hockey practice (which Cissy had somehow talked me into) and working on the school Halloween party, I'd hardly had any time left to think about which Boomerang was my father. One day after school, though, I stopped at the record store and bought a copy of *Sydney Downie Down Down* and took it home and played it on the stereo, listening the way you listen to something you've heard about a million times. I studied the album cover and saw the Boomerangs—Clive, Oscar, Jamie, and Pudge—standing on the Sydney Harbour Bridge in their shorts and shirts and bush hats and holding boomerangs. A boomerang is actually a curved throwing stick used by the aborigines, and I remember reading somewhere that on the cover of the album *Sydney Downie Down Down* the Boomerangs (the group) were trying to represent all aspects of Australia. Another thing about a boomerang is that when you throw it it comes back, and what I think is that the group called themselves the Boomerangs because when they play their music it comes back—in people's heads. I looked at the picture again and saw that Oscar was holding his boomerang up over his head, and that he was holding it in his left hand.

I'm left-handed, too. Hey! I wonder if *that's* hereditary. And there I was, holding my left hand out as if it didn't belong to me. After a while I picked up the album and studied it carefully. Clive and Pudge were out. I stared at Oscar, who all of a sudden looked just like the green-and-yellow toy monkey I'd had as a child. I'd named him Oscar and carried him everywhere. The trouble was that every time I heard the name now, I thought of that monkey—which I guess means that Oscar's a good name for a monkey but not for a father.

And that left Jamie, which was okay because I liked Jamie. I liked his looks and his music and the fact that he was called the "serious Boomerang." I'm serious myself (sometimes, anyway). "Jamie Ward," I said out loud. "Sydney Ward. Sydney Downie Ward. Sydney Downie Cellar Door Ward." Talk about a pleasing-sounding name. My grade school teacher should've heard *that*.

I flipped the record over and listened to Jamie singing "Every Morning," leaning closer to make sure of the words. When I heard him singing to someone called "Little Lovey" I got this weird-all-over feeling. I mean, could he be singing to *my mother*?

I turned back to side one and found "In the Land of Never Never," which, even though I've never been in love (Jeff Clark when I was in eighth grade doesn't really count), I still think has to be one of the greatest love songs ever written. I cranked up the volume because some things you just have to listen to loud, no matter what ~~Mom says~~ Mrs. Hubbard says. I closed my eyes, mouthing the words.

The music swelled and Jamie's voice grew stronger, louder, and sort of throbbing.

And just then *thump thump thump* came Mrs. Hubbard's broom on her ceiling down below, and I could tell she was into being a landlady.

Mrs. Hubbard, Extended

The most important thing about Mrs. Hubbard, more important than the cats and the birds, is that she is a hypocrite. I'm not saying this to be mean or anything but because she is. In fact, she's one of those people who lives by the letter of the law even while she's breaking it.

The explanation for this is that we live in the kind of neighborhood where it's against the law to make your house into apartments (it's not exactly a law but a covenant, which is sort of the same thing). Apparently, the people who originally built these houses were sort of snotty (Freudian slip—I meant snooty) and couldn't imagine anyone not being able to afford anything. But when Mr. Hubbard died, Mrs. Hubbard needed some extra money to be able to stay in her house, so she told her friend Birdy-Morrison (who had just hired a new

young teacher with a baby) that she was looking for someone to "share" her home.

Enter Mom and me.

The trouble is that "sharing" someone's home isn't the
same as really living in it. "Sharing" someone's home
isn't the same as having your own front door and your
own lock and key. What we <u>do</u> have is a chunk of Mrs.
Hubbard's second floor: two bedrooms, with a bath in
between, and a sort of living room in an enclosed upstairs
porch, which you have to go out into the hall to get to.
The worst part is that we have to use Mrs. Hubbard's
kitchen, and even though we've always had our own
shelves and our own space in the refrigerator, this gave
me a lot of trouble when I was little: I was forever eating
up her stewed prunes, and once a whole salmon mousse
she had made for her bridge club.

Other disadvantages of "sharing" someone's home are
having to get dressed just to go down to the kitchen, never
being able to have a party, or a dog either. Whenever I
try to talk to Mom about getting a place of our own, she
says, "Well, this is not ideal, but it's okay for now."
(Except that "for now" has spanned my entire life.) Needless to say, it's not <u>exactly</u> Mrs. Hubbard's fault that my
mother is in a rut. When I was little I used to hope that
a prince would come along and sweep her off her feet.
But that was before I figured out about her and the
Boomerang.

Anyway, Mrs. Hubbard usually tries to pretend we're

*not here (the way she pretends that the envelope my
mother leaves propped against the sugar bowl in the
kitchen on the first of every month isn't really the rent),
but when she does think of us it's as poor but honest
relatives she's taken under her wing. I mean, once I came
home from school and interrupted her bridge club. As I
was going up the stairs, I heard her saying, "My niece's
child, you know. I've had them here for years."*

*Which all has to do with why Mom and I ended up
with an apartment that isn't quite an apartment and a
landlady who doesn't think she is one.*

Notes from Sam Klemkoski to Sydney Downie: (1) *If
it's "needless to say," don't say it.* (2) <u>*Don't*</u> *sell your
mother short. Besides, there are more frogs than princes,
or even Boomerangs.*

Observation from Sydney Downie to herself (to be
marked as private with a paper clip): *Frogs? Princes?
Boomerangs? Sam Klemkoski and* <u>*my mother*</u>*?*

Halloween is a big deal at Hawthorne Hills. What
happens is that on Halloween day we all go home right
after school so we can work on our costumes (except that
everybody's *been* working on them for ages), and then we
all come back that night for a party in the Big Hall. This
year Cissy, Mary Jo, and I decided to be something together and we spent ages thinking of things that came in

threes: Three Blind Mice, the Three Little Pigs, or even Wynken, Blynken, and Nod. Then one day, when we were more stuck than usual, I said, "How about the Boomerangs?"

"We can't—there were four of them," said Mary Jo.

"We'll get Winkle Shultz," I said. "She doesn't know what to be and every time she mentions it her mother tells her to be a gypsy." (Mothers *always* say to be gypsies for Halloween.)

"Only if I can be Pudge," said Cissy, drumming on her E.T. notebook with a pencil.

"And I'm Clive," said Mary Jo, pushing up her glasses.

"And I'll be either Oscar or Jamie, whichever Winkle doesn't want," I said, trying to sound noble even though I was *sure* she'd pick Oscar. That's on account of Jamie being the quiet one and Winkle being anything *but* quiet.

Winkle said yes, *and* she chose Oscar, *and* she said we could use her brothers' old guitars and a broken-down drum stored in her attic. We bought four cheapo boomerangs (the toy kind, not the weapons), and for costumes we decided to wear camp shorts, shirts, knee socks, and cowboy hats with the crowns pushed down and sort of flat. There wasn't much we could do with our hair, but at least mine was the right color, and the rest decided to keep their hats on a lot. The whole time we were working on our costumes in Cissy's family room I kept thinking about my mother, wondering what she'd think when she saw us, and would it make her happy or sad. I made up my mind that no matter how much was going on at the party, I'd never once take my eyes off her face. I mean, how often do you get to see your own mother when the ghost of your own father appears?

The party was great, with lots of guys, food, noise, music, and some pretty wild costumes—but no prizes. There never are, at Hawthorne Hills, because what Birdy-Morrison wants is for us to do things for the "joy of doing them, girls." If there *had* been a prize for the best teacher's costume, though, I'd've given it to Maddie Stephens, who was an overdue library book. Sam came as a tree (I guess to remind us that he's really a wood sculptor at heart), and my mother as a gypsy.

The big thing was that we (the Boomerangs, I mean) got to perform. We had taken along a tape of "Avago," set the tape player up on the stairs, and stood in front of it, mouthing the words and miming on the instruments. The only trouble was that by the time I remembered my mother and looked out to see how she was reacting, the walls of the Big Hall were vibrating and everybody around us was rocking and shouting and chanting "A—va—go . . ." And Mom was nowhere in sight.

November

I spent the night after the Halloween party at Cissy's, so it wasn't till the next day (Saturday) that I got around to asking my mother how she'd liked our act, and she said she hadn't seen it because we went on just about the time she was outside trying to keep a crowd of boys from Milton High from sneaking beer into the party.

"Do you know who we went as?" I asked.

"Why do people keep asking me that?" she said. "First Sam, and then Maddie Stephens, and now you. Of course I do. You were some rock group."

"The Boomerangs, Mom. You know, the Boomerangs." (The thing about my mother is, I'm never sure when she's consciously putting me on.)

"Oh, yes, the Boomers," she said, laughing in that pale sort of way that lets me know she's slipping into what I call her "mother act." "I remember the Boomers."

"You do?" My voice squeaked and I swallowed hard. "You do."

"Yes. All that hair that was long in back. And those clothes—the Akubra hats, the shorts called stubbies."

"Yes?"

"All that energy." And before I had a chance to find out what was coming next she whisked a sponge mop out of the closet and said, "Well, put all that energy to good use and do the bathroom floor, please."

And she was gone, down the steps and on her way to the store. One thing I have to give her—my mother's not a fanatic when it comes to cleaning (Mary Jo's mother claims that any floor that's not scrubbed on your hands and knees isn't scrubbed at all). So it didn't take me long to finish. I stood for a while afterward, looking at the cracked tiles and the feet on the bathtub and the way the grout along the top of the sink had turned a disgusting green, and wondering about Mom. Was she really in such a hurry to get to the store, or was it all a defense? I mean, did just thinking about her Boomerang years fill her with angst? (That's a word I heard Sam use once and I'm not sure I have it just right.)

Later that afternoon I was over at the Martins', baby-sitting for Porter and helping myself to his trick-or-treat bag. We'd already weeded out the awful stuff—unwrapped cookies, hard candies fuzzed with lint, and Baggies of popcorn—and had started in on the miniature Snickers and Milky Ways.

"I have to do a room," I said.

"Room smoom."

"For creative writing. I mean, we have to describe a room so that the person *reading* about it will know something about the person *living* in it without ever having met him. Or her."

"Oh," said Porter, peeling the paper off a Tootsie pop as he said, "You could use mine."

"Yeah," I said, pulling in my arms and legs to keep from being eaten alive by grunge. I was sitting on the floor on top of what was probably a pile of clean laundry, except that in Porter's room it's hard to tell, and thinking how maybe his mother shouldn't have bothered. I mean, underneath the trucks and cars, the five thousand Lincoln Logs, the birds' nests, rocks, and empty jars and bottles, I could see the traces of a little boy's room. You know, the kind you see in a magazine, with bunk beds and circus wallpaper.

"You *could*," Porter said again.

"Yeah, well, it smells, sort of," I said, switching from Milky Ways to sour balls, on the theory that just plain sugar wasn't as bad for my skin as chocolate.

"That's just the banana," he said, reaching under the

bed for a bowl of mush with greenish-blackish mold growing on top. "Unless it's William." He pointed to a gross-
out goldfish floating on his side in a bowl on the bookcase.
"He's dead and I'm waiting to see what happens next."

"What happens next is I leave," I said, getting up and
running for the door. "There's something about your
room that doesn't lend itself to description. How about
your brother's? You know, your brother the Boomerang
freak."

"Wally?"

"Yeah."

"Wally Smally," said Porter.

Wally's Room

*Wally's room is on the third floor of the Martins' house
(the other rooms up there are guest rooms), and since
he's away at school and there aren't any guests, that part
of the house doesn't look at all like the downstairs part,
which is expensive casual. I mean, Mrs. Martin has a
decorator and a plant person (not a gardener, but an inside
person who comes once a week to "do" the plants). And
because of the way the Martins are always leaving empty
glasses and half-eaten sticky buns and tennis racquets all
over everything, she also has Maisie, who comes in and
cleans it all up (except that she won't set foot in Porter's
room).*

Wally's room is large, with the roof making slanty,

angly places that are cool to look at and dangerous to your head, and the thing is, it's obvious that, even from his boarding school in New Hampshire, he managed to keep his mother's decorator <u>out</u>. I mean, it's Wally's room.

Wally's room has a water bed (which gave me the same feeling I get from sitting on the trampoline, only more so), a funny old dresser with the mirror hooked on, and glass-fronted bookcases all along one wall with books inside and beer cans (empty) lined up on the top. And the walls (even the slanted parts that are half roof and half wall) are covered with Boomerang stuff.

I mean, Wally Martin, who lives in the house right in back of mine (except that he's never there) and whose little brother I baby-sit for, is a real genuine Boomerang freak.

I twisted around on the water bed so I could see all his things: the pictures and the posters, the Boomerang beach towel stretched end to end, the official coloring book open to a picture of Oscar brushing his hair, a plastic Boomerang mask and Halloween costume (which was what Mrs. Hubbard calls store-bought and not as good as ours). And hanging from the ceiling on a piece of string, a "Wombat Walk" lunch box.

"Wow," I said, reaching for the trick-or-treat bag Porter had brought along and popping a Reese's Peanut Butter Cup in my mouth. "But what I don't understand is how come he doesn't have all this stuff with him at school."

*"Because he's dumb," said Porter, pushing himself up
into a headstand against the door.*
"Dumb smumb," he said in an upside-down voice.

Note from Sam Klemkoski to Sydney Downie: *Show,
don't tell. Let the room speak for itself. And "real genuine"
is a redundancy.*

Well, of course I knew that—about "real genuine," I
mean—but sometimes drastic measures are called for.
Anyway, the second-neatest thing about Wally Martin's
room (the first being just the fact of its existence) was that
Porter told me I could borrow some things.

"Oh, I couldn't," I said, flipping through the records
and reaching out to touch the Boomerang books.

"Could smould," said Porter. "But only if you hurry,
'cause there's nothing to do up here, and besides that you
said you'd play me a game of checkers."

"Maybe *Wombat Walk*, then. And *Ayers Rock Rock*,
too. But I'll have them back before Wally comes home
for Thanksgiving."

"You don't have to," said Porter. "He won't *be* here
for Thanksgiving."

And for a minute I got this really creepy feeling that
maybe there wasn't any such person as Wally Martin; or
that maybe a long time ago he'd run away or been kid-
napped or something, and the family just kept his room

the way it was the last time he'd used it (like Mrs. Hubbard and Dimples, sort of).

"He's meeting us in Vermont and we're all going skiing for Thanksgiving," said Porter, and I figured even the Martins wouldn't go skiing with someone who didn't exist. I picked up the albums and a couple of books and followed Porter down the stairs, wondering as I went if Mrs. Martin wouldn't like to take me along to help take care of him. When we got to the kitchen, Porter went to look for the checkers and I stood in front of the window and tried to imagine myself poised at the top of a gigantic mountain in Vermont, with the snow and the wind swirling around me. Somehow the picture was slow to come, and I decided that probably what I'd like better was the part afterward, in the lodge, curled up in front of a blazing fire. "Après ski," I think it's called. The whole time Porter was setting up the board I thought how he was really lucky. I mean, anything would be better than *our* typical Thanksgiving at Hawthorne Hills.

For the next few days, I kept thinking about Wally's room and how it wasn't fair that it was his and not mine. I mean, he wasn't even *there*. And besides, *I* was the one with Boomerang blood (maybe). Sometimes at night I would lie on my bed looking at my room and trying to figure what somebody else looking at it would learn about me. I decided they'd think I was a really blah person, which I'm not (but the furniture belongs to Mrs. Hubbard, so what can you expect?). I also decided that Porter's room said some really gross things and that Porter wasn't gross at all, so maybe Sam's theory of learning about a person from his/her room was false. (And I wondered what his room said about him.)

Speaking of Sam, lately he'd really been talking about similes and metaphors a lot. ("They're like spices," he said, "and you have to use them sparingly.") The thing is, I thought of one (simile, I think), and even though I don't know if it'll work I'll try it anyway.

You know how crickets make that dreadful racket on hot summer days and sometimes the noise gets louder and louder and sort of throbs? Well, that's what it's like at school now. Only, instead of crickets I'm talking teachers, and instead of noise I'm talking work. But the result's the same: frenzy. (Except that everybody pretends it isn't happening, because Hawthorne Hills is supposed to be such a laid-back place.)

The thing that bugs me the most about teachers is the way they think each student takes just one course. Theirs. And Sam was the worst. I mean, we wrote and revised and wrote some more. We wrote about rooms and schools and people we did and didn't know; about where we'd been and where we'd like to go.

And every time we complained Sam just smiled and said, "Writers write."

The one time I griped to my mother she hardly looked

up from the papers she was marking as she said, "Heavens, Sydney, the reason you're in that class is that you want to be a writer."

"Not anymore," I said, going into my room and slamming the door, thinking how mothers who are teachers are *much less* sympathetic than mothers who aren't, and that it was obvious I'd been right all along about Sam not being Carol Weatherby and that maybe he should stick to wood carving. The next day I went to the library and got a pamphlet out of the vertical file called *My Career as a Dental Hygienist*.

And then the day after *that*, Sam gave an assignment that made me think I'd been wrong about him all along. That maybe he really was a caring, sensitive person. It was an assignment I was sure he'd designed just for me. It was a showcase.

Because that very day Sam stood up in front of the class (actually, he slouched against the door frame) and said, "You'll probably have to do some research for this one, but I want you each to write about your most famous relative."

And right away everybody groaned and rolled their eyes.

Except me. Because who *else* at Hawthorne Hills had a relative who was even a little bit famous?

* * *

It was the kind of project that went well right from the start. The kind where even the research was fun. I had my index cards and on the top one I wrote *Jamie Ward: My Father*. I had the Boomerang books I'd gotten out of the library and from Wally Martin's room, and now, instead of trying to squeeze the time I spent reading them in *around* my homework, they *were* my homework. The only trouble was trying to decide what to leave out. (Sam has a real thing about papers that are too long—I think because he has to read them.) I mean, if I threw in that Jamie loves fishing and surfing and being lazy sometimes for a whole day at a time, then I probably wouldn't have room for the fact that he hates tea with sugar or that his favorite color is green. If I wrote too much about the early years, there wouldn't be enough space for the Boo-merang years, or even for the time after the group disbanded.

Finally, on a night when my mother had gone to the movies with Maddie Stephens, I shuffled my index cards one more time and settled down on the bed to write. But what I can't figure out is why something that'd gone so well all along suddenly didn't. I'm talking big-time stuck. It's not that I didn't write *anything*, because I did. A line, maybe two. Then I'd cross out what I'd written, bunch up the paper and throw it on the floor, and start again. Except every time I stopped and started up again, I must have used what I already had and added on to it, because all of a sudden I was done. And there I was surrounded by about a hundred balls of paper, the way real writers always are—in movies, anyway.

Then I pushed my pillows higher in back of me and started to read, pretending, the way I do sometimes, that what I've written has nothing to do with me and that I'm seeing it for the first time.

Jamie Ward: My Father

My father, Jamie Ward, was born in Sydney, Australia, on September 5, 1947, and was the youngest of three children (and the youngest Boomerang). His father was a butcher and his mother, who was jolly and outgoing, was a teacher and did a lot to encourage her son in his musical career. In fact, she gave him his first guitar and often listened to him practice all night long. (In the beginning, when I was struggling to find out which Boomerang was my father, it was the things I read about Margaret Ward that helped me decide. I mean, anybody who would listen to someone teaching himself to play the guitar practice all night is the kind of grandmother I want. Besides that, she spends most of her time now answering letters from Jamie's fans, and someday, in the fullness of time, I'll probably write to her myself. Not as a fan but as a granddaughter.)

Jamie's first school was Paddington Primary, and right from the start he was a good student. Next he went to the local high school, where he met Clive, Oscar, and

Pudge. From then on, he was mostly interested in surfing and playing his guitar. One year during his vacation he went into the outback and worked on a cattle station.

So many things happened to the Boomerangs in the late 1960s and the early seventies that it's hard to know what to include. But I guess that's what Boomerang Madness is all about. In the fall of 1968, they toured the United States and ended up doing a concert at the White House for the President. And two years later, they were given medals by the Queen of England.

But for Jamie I'm sure none of that could compare to the time when he met a young graduate student from the United States named Martha Foley. After a whirlwind courtship, Jamie and Martha were married, and in the fullness of time a child was born. (Me.)

But sadly, things have a habit of not staying the same. As time went by, the Boomerangs split up and each went his own way. Tragically, Jamie and Martha also split up, and Martha took the baby (me) and returned to her own country, resigned to living out the rest of her life alone, with just her daughter. Eventually she has managed to suppress her Boomerang years, though I am sure she will never forget them.

It's fun to have a famous father. It's fun to read about him in books, to see his picture, and to listen to him sing and play his guitar. And sometimes, in the early evening, I step outside, scanning the sky for the first star and wishing on it—that someday my father and I will meet.

Who'd've ever thought that one class could come up with so many famous relatives? And the way Sam took forever giving those papers back, reading them out loud, and then commenting, I thought he was never going to get to mine. First, there was Winkle Shultz's grandfather who had been a judge and Mary Jo's great-uncle by marriage who was once the governor. Milly Blunt had a relative way back during the Civil War who was a runaway slave and had escaped to Canada by way of the Underground Railroad, and the totally weird thing was that someone in Janet Preller's family was one of the Quakers who'd *helped* the slaves escape. That's when things got really bogged down. I mean, Sam got so into the coincidence of it all and how it's possible that Janet's kin had helped Milly's kin and that maybe it had been preordained for Janet and Milly to meet years later at Hawthorne Hills.

While this was going on, I kept trying to see my own paper in the stack and figured that Sam was saving the best for last—but if he didn't hurry, class'd be over.

He didn't and it was. And then, when everybody was drifting out of the room, he came up and slipped me my paper without saying anything.

Note from Sam Klemkoski to Sydney Downie: *We'll get to fantasy. Maybe you can recycle this and use it later.*

Observation from Sydney Downie to herself: *I hate Sam Klemkoski.*

* * *

And I did. I hated him all the way home after school (where I scooped up my baby-sitting money and a Boomerang picture) and the whole way over to the mall. I hated him as I sat in the chair at the Hair Snippery and watched in the mirror as some girl cut my hair short on the sides and spiked my bangs and I saw myself turning into a Boomerang look-alike.

("Hey, that looks cute on you," the girl said as she brushed powder on my neck.)

("It's uneven" is what my mother said.)

And I hated him the next day back in class as I sat there with my Boomerang haircut and my Boomerang blood boiling inside of me.

I mean, I was mad. And not only at Sam. I was mad at my friends, too (for not understanding why I was mad at Sam), and at my mother (for marrying a Boomerang— or not marrying one, I wasn't sure which). And I was mad at the university student named Arthur Downie (if there was such a person).

By the time Thanksgiving came, I still wasn't feeling much better. I mean, Porter was away, so I wasn't making any money baby-sitting, and Cissy's sisters were home from college and she didn't want to do anything but hang out with them, and Mary Jo's grandparents had come from Oregon and her mother made her stick around so she could help entertain. And then, when we got to

Hawthorne Hills (where all the strays of the world unite for Thanksgiving dinner), my mother kept watching the door as if she was waiting for someone, and I had this hideous feeling it might be Sam, only he didn't come and eventually she stopped watching. The only good things about the day were the weird things that happened: Birdy-Morrison dozed off when she was supposed to be carving the turkey, the pumpkin pie tasted of chalk dust, and Mademoiselle (the French teacher) brought the same fish soup she'd brought last year and nobody liked it any better *this* year. I figured I could use them when Sam assigned his "How I Spent My Thanksgiving Holiday" paper.

He didn't, though. Instead, on the Monday after Thanksgiving, he told us to take out a piece of paper and write two paragraphs on "How I *Wish* I'd Spent My Thanksgiving Holiday."

Okay. If he wanted make-believe I'd give it to him, I thought as I closed my eyes and saw myself again on the ski slopes of Vermont. But not with Porter Martin. Or his family either. This time it was just me and somebody tall and blond and awesomely handsome.

But when it came right down to it, I couldn't. I mean, it may sound weird and I'm sort of embarrassed to say this, but there's something special about Thanksgiving and I never wanted to joke about it.

How I <u>Wish</u> I'd Spent
My Thanksgiving Holiday

I wish I'd spent my Thanksgiving holiday in the middle of a long-distance telephone commercial. You know, the kind you see on television with a mother and a father, kids, and grandparents and aunts and uncles and cousins all seated around this enormous table with a turkey and cranberry sauce and pumpkin pie. Where afterward everybody plays touch football on the lawn, or takes a walk, or just sits in front of the fire and does nothing until it's time for turkey sandwiches.

I wish I'd spent my Thanksgiving holiday in the middle of a long-distance telephone commercial—the kind that, when you first see it, you pretend is going to make you throw up, but then you notice a lump in your throat and it has nothing to do with barfing. Any more than your eyes watering has to do with the cat.

December

Ever since Thanksgiving, it seemed that Sam had been not quite with it. For example, he gave us *fewer* things to write and *more* time to write them in, and the topics he gave us to write *about* were even worse than they'd been before ("Autumn," "Spring," "The Inside of the Classroom")—almost as if he was making them up as he went along. Sometimes he even Xeroxed stories out of books, and we sat around in a circle and talked about mood and theme and what the author intended: the kind of stuff that ruins a good story and makes it almost like meeting a skeleton when you're expecting a real person.

When he finally got around to giving our Thanksgiving pieces back, he had scrawled a poem on the back of mine.

I stood in the doorway, while everybody pushed past me, trying to decipher his handwriting and what he meant by what he had written.

> *Holidays should be like this,*
> *Free from overemphasis,*
> *Time for soul to stretch and spit*
> *Before the world comes back on it.*

"It's not original," he said, throwing open the window to get rid of the stale classroom smell. "Not with me, anyway. But I just wanted you to bear in mind that those long-distance television commercials aren't always all they're cracked up to be."

"Yeah, I guess," I said, rereading the poem and kind of liking the part about stretching and spitting. I shoved the paper in my knapsack and had already started down the hall, when Sam called to me. "Do you have a class now, Sydney?"

"No, I'm just going down to the Big Hall and see who's around."

"Well, come back for a minute, then. There's something I've been meaning to talk to you about."

But when I went back, it was as though Sam had forgotten he'd called me. He sat staring at his hands, picking at the edges of a Band-Aid, and when he spoke, it was more to himself than to me. "Sculptor's hands," he said. "Though they won't be for long, if I don't get back to it." Then he shook his head and said, "Now about this Boomerang business."

"What Boomerang business?"

"Well, your famous-relative paper, for starters." He waited for a moment, and when I didn't say anything, he continued. "And the whole aura that seems to surround you these days."

I crossed my arms over my chest and glowered at him from under my Boomerang bangs. "I did it. What you said—"

"I know what I said, and what I wanted, and what I didn't expect." Sam shook his head again and then went on. "Maybe it was a poor choice of words. Maybe I should've said 'distinctive.' 'Write about your most *distinctive* relative.' "

"It would've still been the same," I said.

"Not necessarily. Distinctive could be your Great-aunt Milly, who just might be a world-class kleptomaniac."

"I don't have one."

"Well, your Aunt Agnes the tightrope walker, then. Or your Uncle Wilburforce, who makes time bombs in the basement."

"I don't have one of those either," I said. "Besides, I happen to have a perfectly good father that I wrote a perfectly good piece about."

"And *I* happen to be a bit of a Boomerang aficionado myself, and I've never seen any mention of a Martha Downie or a Martha Foley or a Martha anything else."

"And everybody knows that *some* things are too *private* to mention," I said as I got up and headed for the door, scrunching my shoulders and waiting for him to bellow after me. (I mean, at Hawthorne Hills we're supposed to be able to say almost anything, but I wasn't sure Sam understood that.)

And he did bellow. His voice rose and rolled and bounced off the walls of that second-floor hall and stuck in my ears for the rest of the day. "Well, Miss Sydney Downie Down Down, if that's the case, then your chronology's off by a mile. Unless you're a lot older than I think you are. And *furthermore*, if you ever want to talk, you know where to find me."

I hate Sam Klemkoski.

Just when I was beginning to feel a tiny bit sorry for him for having to teach us when I knew he'd rather be sculpting (the way I feel sorry for myself for having to do history, instead of writing in my journal), he had to go and spoil it all. "Boomerang business"—ha! "If you ever want to talk"—double ha! I'd sooner talk to Godzilla, or that peculiar Fiona Finch, the guidance counselor that nobody *ever* wants to talk to.

But the awful thing is that he was right about the chronology. I don't know how I could've messed up, except that with all the fuss about Boomerang Madness, I guess I just wanted to be a part of it. Anyway, I got out my Boomerang books and started over, working it out like one of those math problems we used to have in grade school. You know, if a train from New York, going eighty miles per hour, passes a train from Baltimore, going ninety miles per hour, then how many apples are in Farmer Brown's orchard? (Or something like that.)

Question: If Jamie Ward met and married Martha Foley in 1967 (the year the Boomerangs played two engagements in London and were on the top of the charts more than they weren't), and if they had me right away (so that I just might've managed to be around for the night when the boys played at this humongous concert that stopped traffic in downtown Sydney almost forever), how old would that make me now? Answer: twenty-two. Which I'm not.

Question: If Jamie Ward met and married Martha Foley in 1970 (the year the Boomerangs took off across Australia, even up into the Northern Territory), and if they had me right away (so I'd've been around the next year by the time "Wombat Walk" reached number one not only in Australia but in Britain and America as well), how old would I be now? Answer: nineteen. Which I'm not.

But I was getting closer. The only thing was that it gave me a sort of crawly feeling to try to figure out when I was conceived.

But to get on with it.

Question: If Jamie Ward met and married Martha

Foley early in 1974, and if they had me right away, then that would make me fifteen—which I am. But 1974? What was so special about 1974? And what were the Boomerangs doing then? For a minute I felt disappointed, and cheated, and like I'd gotten to the theater when the play was already over. I picked up another book, opening it to the back: the part that had dates, lists of albums, and a bibliography.

By 1974, Clive had disappeared, Oscar was making movies, Pudge had moved to the U.K., and Jamie was living in the outback and trying to get in touch with the music of the Aborigines.

It sounded boring at first (the outback and the music of the Aborigines), and nothing to compare with tours and concerts and crowds waiting in the streets. As though it had all been a hoax and *Sydney Downie Down Down* had really been a downer. But the more I thought about it, the more I thought it might be okay (the outback and the Aborigines). That it was somehow mysterious and cosmic and simple and complicated, all at the same time.

It wasn't long after this that Sam gave his prize-winning assignment. He started out by saying there was nothing that did more for a writer's ego than to be in print. Then he went on about how one of the easiest ways to break into print was through the "Letters to the Editor" of a newspaper. *Then* he explained how we were all going to write letters to the editor of the *Sun*, and if anyone actually got her letter in the paper, he'd give her a prize. (Prize-winning assignment!)

"Make the subject of your letter something you really care about," he said. "A cause, if you will. Or a strong opinion you want to express, a position you wish to defend." Sam stood up and sort of stretched as he said, "And to show how important I think this is, I'm willing to give up valuable class time so we can all go down to the library and you can start searching for a topic." (Of course, being the daughter of a teacher, I know the old trick of taking the class to the library during "valuable class time": it means the teacher's either unprepared or frazzled.)

"What d'ya think the prize is?" said Cissy as we all tromped off to the library.

"I'll bet it's nothing special," said Mary Jo. "Probably a used book the library doesn't want anymore."

"Yeah," I said. "You know the old Do-it-for-the-glory-of-winning thing."

"Except that it *would* be sort of nice. Getting something I'd written in the newspaper," said Cissy.

"Or something *I'd* written," I said.

"Or me," said Mary Jo.

"Even if it *was* just a letter to the editor," said Cissy.

"I'd rather it was a poem," said Mary Jo.

"Or maybe a story," I said.

"But just to be *in print*," we all said, sighing deeply.

In print. Just the thought of it made me feel light-headed, and I decided not to rush into becoming a dental hygienist. Not yet, anyway.

Even with all the classes Sam was willing to give up in the interest of our letters, I wasn't doing well. For someone who feels intensely, my mind was a blank. I didn't have a cause, an opinion, or a position, but what I did have was a headache from reading about teachers' salaries, the environment, AIDS, graffiti on public buildings, the Middle East, white-collar crime, and unemployment. I thought of writing about saving the whales, but then I noticed that Winkle Shultz had two whale books and a bunch of *National Geographics* piled up in front of her, and I decided to bag that idea.

I remembered how Sam'd said he was so sure we'd do well with our letters that we didn't even have to show him the rough drafts (that we could just go ahead and mail them ourselves), and I figured that if I didn't do mine he'd never know and would just think the *Sun* decided not to print it. Except that I'd know. (Besides that, the honor code's a pretty big deal at Hawthorne Hills.)

And just when I was beginning to feel as if I was racing against the egg timer in Mrs. Hubbard's kitchen, with the sand running out faster than I could think, I got an idea. And in a weird sort of way it was Sam Klemkoski who gave it to me when he returned my famous-relative piece. Sam, who'd said that maybe I could recycle what I'd already written.

The first I knew about my letter being in the paper was when Porter came pounding on the kitchen door one morning about a week later, just as I was pouring myself a bowl of Spoon Size Shredded Wheat. When I opened the door he shoved a bunched-up section of newspaper at me, said "Paper smaper," and "Car pool smar pool," then took off through the hedge and down his driveway to a waiting station wagon, where somebody's mother was leaning on the horn.

When I went to spread the paper out on the kitchen table, I was so excited my hands were shaking, and for a minute I just stood there, looking down at the whole page: the editorials, the cartoon (the kind that has to do with politics and not comics), and a whole big chunk headed LETTERS TO THE EDITOR. There, in the lower right-hand corner, was my letter. With its own headline.

BOOMERANG BLOOD

I caught my breath and sat down hard and had to wait awhile before I could begin to read.

Editor:
I thought it might be of interest to you and your readers that during the time known as Boomerang Madness, a

local young woman met and married one of the Boomerangs: Jamie Ward, my father. And because my
mother (the local young woman who is now a local middle-aged woman) has always been a very private person,
and because my father—even though *he* lived in a goldfish bowl—respected that privacy, she managed to keep
her secret for many years.

It's only because I am a student at Hawthorne Hills
School, where the entire student body is studying self-
awareness, that I made my discovery. I learned that my
father was born in Sydney to hardworking and encour-
aging parents; that while he was in school he met up
with Clive, Oscar, and Pudge; and that eventually they
went on to fame and fortune.

I am proud that the Boomerangs are part of my her-
itage, and part of my blood.

> Sincerely yours,
> *Sydney Downie*

Sydney Downie. My name in print. My letter in print,
with every word just the way I'd written it. A warm,
bubbly feeling started at my feet and began working its
way up through my body. It had gotten about as far as
my elbows when my mother dashed into the kitchen,
poured coffee into a mug, and headed for the back door.

"Mom, look what Porter brought over. Look what I—"

"Sorry, Sydney," she said, "but I'm supposed to meet
a student for a conference before school and I'm running
late. Come on."

Now, the thing is, my mother takes student conferences

very seriously, and whatever she is *very serious* about she is also *single-minded* about. So I folded the paper and slipped it into my knapsack, figuring I'd tell her about it that night and meanwhile I'd spend the day feeling warm and bubbly—and proud.

What I hadn't figured on was how many people read the "Letters to the Editor" in the *Sun.* I mean, no sooner had Mom parked the car and taken off for her appointment than it started. I was just getting my stuff out of the backseat when Maddie Stephens pulled up next to me, rolled down her window, and said, "Way to go, Sydney," with an I-knew-about-it-all-along look on her face. Cissy and Mary Jo saw me and came charging up the driveway, screaming "Congratulations" and pounding me on the back (which was really nice of them, especially since I'm sure deep down they couldn't help wishing one of *their* letters had been used). Of course, I said that maybe theirs'd be in tomorrow or the next day, though secretly deep down I was hoping they wouldn't and that mine would be the only one. That made me feel mean. And not like a good friend at all. Then the captain of the hockey team punched me on the arm and said, "Are you for real, Downie?" and three freshmen asked if I could get them autographs.

Birdy-Morrison, when I finally made it into the Big Hall, threw out her arms and stood quivering in her morning-glory dress, saying, "Just think, our own Martha

Downie, our own Sydney." Then she told me to remind my mother to bring creamed onions for Christmas dinner at Hawthorne Hills again this year.

Sam was ready for me when I got to creative writing later that morning. He had Scotch-taped the whole page from the newspaper to the middle of the blackboard, and next to it, in yellow chalk, he'd written *Congratulations, Sydney*. Then there was an asterisk, and at the very bottom of the board he'd added *I guess* in cramped little letters, which I thought was a really negative comment and not likely to do much for my warm, bubbly feeling.

When we'd all settled down, Sam said he thought maybe it was time for us to have a discussion about "responsibility" and "accurate research"—even if they were just letters to the editor we had written. (Just letters to the editor!) With that, everybody groaned and slid lower in their chairs, and it turned out to be a sort of patchy discussion, the kind that's made up of a lot of empty spaces the teacher hopes the kids will eventually fill in with significant "contributions," but nobody ever does.

"What's Sydney's prize, though?" Cissy finally asked during one of the lulls.

"Ah, a pragmatist in our midst," said Sam, and when Cissy looked at him blankly, he just nodded toward the dictionary and went on. "Because I don't want to encourage anyone's baser and more materialistic instincts, and because of my own penurious position, Sydney's prize, and anyone else's whose letter is published, will be a visit, with a friend of her choice, to an artist's studio. Mine."

I'd rather have a used library book, wrote Mary Jo on a scrap of paper she pushed in my direction.

"A light meal is also included," said Sam.

"Sounds like an airplane flight—food and beverages will be served aloft," whispered Cissy as she leaned down to tie her shoe.

I'd hardly had time to think about this when my mother appeared at the door, beckoning to me. She dragged me down the hall to the teachers' room, shaking her fist and sputtering all the way. Fiona Finch, who was half buried under a stack of manila folders, took one look at the two of us and scurried out the door, the funny nibbly look on her face making me think of a rat deserting a sinking ship.

And if I was the ship, I was sinking fast.

"Sydney Ann Downie, just *what* do you think you're doing?" my mother said.

"Well—"

"And *who* do you think you are?"

"That's just what I—"

"I'm waiting for an explanation."

"It has to do with my self-awareness," I began.

"What about *my* self-awareness? What about your telling the world that I was married to some rock star?"

"Jamie, Mom. Jamie Ward."

"How *dare* you embarrass me like this! And what about your father's memory. Your *real* father, not some . . . some . . ."

"Boomerang," I said.

"Don't comment," she said, and I wondered what'd happened to the good old Hawthorne Hills emphasis on freedom of expression.

"What do you have to say for yourself, young lady?" my mother went on, shaking the morning paper at me. Her copy looked worn and tattered.

For a minute I started to remind her that she'd told me not to comment, but I thought better of it.

"I'm waiting," she said.

"Only that—"

"And what's more"—her voice peaked on the "more"—"how *dare* you call me *middle-aged!*"

Just then there was a knock on the door and Fiona Finch pushed it open, saying that a reporter from the *Sun* wanted an interview with me, and maybe a picture.

"Oh no they don't," screamed my mother, hurling herself in front of me just as the flashbulb went off and squiggles of light spun out from the corners of my eyes.

The picture was on the front page of the local section of the paper that afternoon. Mom and I looked like a pair of sumo wrestlers in drag. The caption said: "Sydney

Downie, a student at Hawthorne Hills School, claims to be the daughter of former Boomerang Jamie Ward. Her mother would not comment."

I hardly need to put down what supper was like in our house that night. I mean, my mother, who's not usually into feeling sorry for herself, sighed a lot. She moaned. She started all her sentences with "I've done the best I could, but . . ." She shook her head and said (instead of *to* me it was more like *at* me) that students in her class had spent the day asking her about Ayers Rock and the Billabong Club and if she'd ever had a song written just for her—and what was *she* supposed to say to *that?*

She went on so much that it reminded me of the time, years ago, when I broke Mrs. Hubbard's cookie jar and crossed my heart about a million times that I hadn't, and she said something about a lady protesting too much.

And finally, to try and change the subject, I told Mom how Birdy-Morrison told me to remind her to be sure and bring creamed onions for Christmas dinner again this year. And with that, my mother threw a wooden spoon across the kitchen (sending the new tortoiseshell Dimples up the curtain) and said, "I *hate* creamed onions."

It was at that exact moment that I knew how to get my mother out of dinner at Hawthorne Hills—and what to do with Sam's prize.

The next morning I was waiting at the parking lot when Sam's yellow van came gasping up the hill. As we walked along the path to school, I explained to him about Mom and the creamed onions, and Christmas at Hawthorne Hills, and how she'd been feeling a little down lately, anyway."

"Because of the creamed onions?" he said.

"Yes," I said.

"You can't think of any other reason?" he asked.

"Well, you know how it's sometimes the *little* things that get to a person," I said.

"The proverbial straw that breaks the camel's back? Is that it?"

"Yeah," I said. And then I said how maybe if I took my prize on *Christmas* and brought my mother instead of a friend, it might help a little. (Yeah, I know. Sometimes Mom *is* my friend, but definitely not since yesterday.)

We stopped by the bike rack and for a minute Sam stood pulling on his chin. Then he threw back his head and said, "Why not? But I'll tell you one thing, Sydney Downie, being at my place won't be like being in any long-distance telephone commercial you've ever seen."

Convincing Sam was one thing, but my mother was something else. Mom didn't want to go.

"I can't," she said.

"Why not?" I asked.

"Because he didn't ask me," she said.

"He asked me," I said, crossing my fingers behind my back.

"And besides," she said, "it wouldn't be right. Two teachers from the same school, and a small school at that. People might get the wrong impression."

"It's not a *date*." And right about here the going got tricky. I mean, I wanted to tell my mother this was important to me, that it was something I'd won, without actually reminding her of my letter in the newspaper.

"Think of yourself as sort of extra," I said. Mom got a pinched look on her face.

"A chaperone," I said. The pinched look remained.

"A friend," I said all of a sudden. "Sam said with 'a friend of my choice' and you *are* my choice." Mom's face softened a little.

"And anyway," I pushed on, "every year you say that next year we're not eating Christmas dinner at Hawthorne Hills, and here it is 'next year' and we don't have to."

Mom's face looked better than it had since B.L. (before the letter).

"Well . . ." she said, and I grabbed her and hugged her and swung her around the room, which isn't something I do to my mother very often.

Three days later, Mom said yes.

Sam Klemkoski was right about one thing. Being at his place wasn't like any long-distance telephone commercial I'd ever seen. Part of that had to do with Sam's house, which wasn't like any house I'd ever seen either, and just being there gave me a clue as to why he said that where a person lived said something about the person who lived there. I mean, Sam's house was Sam (or Sam was Sam's house, I'm not sure which). In fact, it had started out as a bakery and not as a house at all.

Sam's house was downtown, with a storefront window in the front room that had a crisscross grille over it and a faded, saggy curtain over that. The chairs and sofa were spare and low to the ground, with squashed cushions that looked as if they were used to being sat on. There were books everywhere, and any leftover spaces were filled with things made of wood that gave me a terrific urge to reach for them and run my fingers over them from top to bottom.

And it was cold.

"No central heating," said Sam as he took our coats and dropped them onto a rocking chair.

"None?" said my mother, folding her arms across her chest and rubbing them. I felt sorry for her. I mean, I'd worn jeans and a big sweater and I was cold, but Mom had insisted on wearing a silk dress, on account of it being Christmas and us going out and all (and I could tell already that this wasn't going to be her idea of "out").

"It's healthier this way," said Sam. "Here, try this until you get used to it." He plucked a kind of hairy-looking plaid wool shirt off a hook on the wall and held it out to my mother, who stood there for a minute looking at it as if it might be alive. Then she took a deep breath and put it on, buttoning it all the way to her chin.

"Besides," said Sam, "there're wood stoves down here and gas heaters on the second floor, though I will admit the third floor gets a tad cold in winter." While he was talking, he led the way through a tiny kitchen under the stairs and on into his studio in back.

That was more like nothing I'd ever seen before than anything I'd ever seen. First of all, it was humongous, with a brick floor and a kind of clutter that you could tell was really incredibly organized. There were books on shelves and tools on racks and wood chips in baskets in front of the stove. There was a workbench wedged tightly into one corner, and on the far wall there were shelves made out of weathered boards, with small pieces of sculpture on them. And in the middle of the floor was a great solid piece of wood, just sitting there.

"This is where I spend my time," said Sam, waving in the direction of an old wooden table with a bunch of chairs around it. "I really just wanted the studio, but it came with the house, which was a white elephant and a bargain I couldn't refuse."

Sam showed us around, talking about wood and grain direction and seasoning, and making them sound like something holy. He pointed out saws and adzes and mallets, and when my fingers hovered over the fat, curved shape of a bird, he told me that "sculpture is the art of touch" and to go ahead and touch. And then after a while he went out, and when he came back we ate Chinese food out of cardboard cartons.

Later, while my mother and Sam Klemkoski were sitting around the table drinking tea, I poked around the studio on my own, listening to the music from the stereo in the front room and to Sam talking about the creative process and loneliness and rejection. And the really weird thing was that my mother was answering him as if she'd spent her life listening to that kind of talk and not the boring everyday stuff in the teachers' room at Hawthorne Hills.

What was even weirder was that a small hard nasty lump seemed to be growing inside of me that made me want to remind everybody that we were there because of my prize, and why didn't they shut up and pay attention (to me).

I wandered into the front room and spent a lot of time flipping through Sam's albums. I waited till the record that was already playing was over, took it off, and had just put *Sydney Downie Down Down* on when Sam appeared.

"It's Christmas, Sydney, so give your mother a break," he said, whipping *my* record off and putting a Vivaldi something or other in its place.

* * *

At that moment I disliked Sam Klemkoski intensely, even if it was Christmas.

Though I had to admit that Christmas at his place had been a lot better than Christmas at Hawthorne Hills.

(But it still wasn't the same as a long-distance telephone commercial.)

January

If you ask me, January is one of those months when, instead of one big thing happening (Christmas, the Fourth of July, or even the first day of school), there're a bunch of little things all strung together, like beads on a necklace. And *this* January was no exception.

The first was that Mrs. Hubbard decided to have a party on New Year's Day and she told us (practically at the last minute) that her guests would be going upstairs to leave their "wraps" and she'd hate to see us disturbed, so perhaps it would be better if we made some plans of our own. Translated, that meant "Be out of the house when my company comes, so they won't think that I (1) take in roomers when I'm not supposed to, or (2) didn't invite my poor but honest relatives, who just happen to be staying here, to the party."

I thought we should've refused to go. I mean, this is where we *live*. But my mother (who is sometimes a wimp) said, "Oh, no problem. Sydney and I were planning to be out that afternoon, anyway." And then to me, later, she went on about how the basis of good manners is being considerate of others, and just because Mrs. Hubbard isn't doesn't mean *we* can't be.

I still think my mother is sometimes a wimp.

Which is why we ended up at the movies on New Year's Day. And the really strange part is that afterward, Mom drove to Sam's converted bakery, where Sam was conveniently waiting with more boxes of Chinese food. I couldn't help wondering how and when, since Christmas, this had all been set up, and I thought of that old movie (*The King and I*) where Yul Brynner kept shaking his head and saying, "It's a puzzlement."

Which it was.

A puzzlement.

Besides that, in the time that I've known her, Mom's life has always been pretty much of an open book (which is a polite way of saying nothing ever happened), so it's doubly hard now to think of her having a secret life.

But to get back to New Year's Day. We ate, and listened to music (Beethoven, this time) and the sound of the wind whistling around the corners of the house, and we talked about New Year's resolutions, the movie we'd seen, and Mrs. Hubbard's party. The neat thing was that Sam agreed with me (that we shouldn't've had to clear out), because he banged on the tabletop and said, "For God's sake, Martha, you shouldn't've had to clear out of there. You *live* there."

Then Mom went through her routine about it not being ideal but it was "okay for now." And Sam winked at me and banged on the table again and said, "Yeah, but watch out, because sometimes 'for now' has a habit of getting away from you." (And for a minute I felt warm and okay, even if there wasn't any central heating *and* we'd almost been literally thrown out into the storm by our wicked old landlady who wouldn't admit to being one.)

Then Mom got that tight, thin-lipped look and changed the subject to school stuff, like accreditation and the curriculum.

Boring.

I was looking around for something to do when I noticed that the big piece of wood in the middle of the studio had had some chunks taken out of it since we'd been there before, and I got to thinking about how Sam does the kind of work he does, and if he sort of *sees* a shape inside the wood and then has to figure a way to let it out. And *that* reminded me of when I was little and Cissy and Mary Jo and I would call up drugstores on the telephone, and when somebody answered we'd ask if they had "Prince Albert" in a can, and if the person said yes we'd shriek, "Well, let him out then," and hang up. (Not to be insulting, but Prince Albert is a brand of tobacco.)

Sam saw me looking at the wood, and it was almost as if he knew what I was thinking, because right away he began talking about how sometimes he starts with an idea that he has to let emerge, and other times he starts with the wood and sees where it takes him. I told him about Prince Albert and he slapped his leg and threw back his head and laughed. Then he went on some more about the "mind's hand" and feeling the shape of an idea, but all the time he was talking he kept looking over at the wood and I could tell he'd rather be *working* on it than *talking* about it. Meanwhile, Mom said all the right things, but I think she noticed, too, because before long she got up and said we had to go. Sam didn't tell us not to, and we both could tell he was itching to get back to work. (Which is sometimes the way I feel when I'm in the middle of writing a story and have to stop to answer the phone or do my homework—except for when what I'm writing isn't going well and I *wish* the phone would ring but I know it won't.)

All of this leads me to one of the other January things: I had come to the conclusion that the reason my mother was so good at listening to Sam Klemkoski talking about his sculpture was that she'd had all that practice listening to Jamie and the other Boomerangs. I have this theory that it doesn't matter if a person writes or sings or sculpts or paints—but that the people who *do* those things (writing, singing, sculpting, and painting) all feel the same way about what they're doing, and anybody who was used to talking to a singer would know how to talk (or listen) to a sculptor. Anyway, I didn't really believe my mother when she said she'd never been a Boomerang bride. I mean, who could've been married to somebody named Arthur Downie and not have anything to show for it except one crinkled snapshot. (And me.)

Sam said right at the beginning of the year that our journals were supposed to be written freely and spontaneously and not revised. The trouble is that I've just read over what I've written lately and the way it sounds (to me, pretending to be reading it for the first time) is that, after my mother's explosion the day my Boomerang letter was in the paper, she just settled down, as if everything was okay.

Not true.

Mom and I spent a lot of time after that being careful, and eyeing one another—the way it was with Dimples the time Mrs. Hubbard's daughter brought her cat over and the two of them (the cats, not Mrs. Hubbard and her daughter) just edged around the room and never once turned their backs on each other. But the thing is, my mother believes in putting a good face on things, especially at Christmastime. So, in a sense, life did sort of just go along.

Until after Christmas, when a reporter from the *Sun*

called, probably because they were hard up for news, to see if he could do an interview, and a woman talk-show host wanted me to be on the radio.

Mom answered the phone both times and told them *no*.

Anyway, that particular development was another of the January things.

Along with Sam giving back our journals (which I forgot to mention he'd collected the first day after the Christmas vacation).

When it came time to hand them in, everybody got really nervous. I mean, Sam *had* said to be totally honest, but when a teacher says to be totally honest, just how honest do they expect you to be?

Mary Jo spent all of class that day going back over her journal and inking stuff out. Cissy clutched hers tight and said how *private* everything was. (Cissy's one of my best friends and I never thought she had anything in her life that was all that private, but sometimes you never know—even about your best friends.) And Janet Preller kept waving hers around, saying, "I'll just *die* if he reads this. I mean it's X-rated," but everybody could tell she was dying for him *to* read it. (Janet has this major crush on a jock from Milton High. Talk about fantasy.)

I wasn't much worried, though, because compared to those guys the worst I did was say I hated Sam Klemkoski (and the way I look at it, teachers have to *expect* those things). When we got them back, though, Scotch-taped right there on the inside cover (sort of back-to-back with E.T.) was a message.

Note from Sam Klemkoski to Sydney Downie: *Give me a break—I know Prince Albert is a kind of tobacco. In my day we made random calls, said, "Is your refrigerator running?," and if the person said yes, we shouted, "Catch it quick before it gets away," and then hung up. Which only proves that "Plus ça change, plus c'est la même chose."*

And by the way, Sydney, don't confuse secretiveness and privacy. Allow your mother a little privacy, too, please. Or, as they say in the parlance: Cut her some slack.

Who? Me?
Who? Mom?
(Anyway, can't you always tell that whenever somebody says "By the way," that's what they really meant to say all along and the rest was extra?)
(What did Sam Klemkoski know about my mother's private life?)
(And furthermore—I'm taking Spanish, not French.)

The thing is that nobody thought Sam actually read the journals, because when we handed them in, a bunch of kids did things like turn certain pages upside down, stick other pages together with grape jelly, and even leave hair or lint or toast crumbs somewhere in the middle, and when they came back, everything was *exactly the same*. Then I thought that maybe he'd just read mine, and only the Christmas and New Year's parts—mainly because I was beginning to suspect there was something between my mother and Sam Klemkoski—but the weird thing was that he started dropping journal things into everyday conversations, like "By the way, Cissy, you may think *Gone with the Wind* is the best book ever written, but just wait till you read *Anna Karenina*," and "Did Porter ever get the dead fish out of his room, Sydney?" or "Oh, Winkle, I hope your weekend with your new stepmother went well."

Which leads me to think I'll never figure Sam out.

Then there was Natalie Gatling. And all I can say is, if the other January things were beads on a necklace, she was the clasp. The kind that catches in your hair and pulls, and the main reason that particular January will be stuck in my mind forever.

So—enter Natalie Gatling, who arrived at Hawthorne Hills on a Wednesday toward the end of January, stood for a minute in the doorway of the Big Hall wrinkling her nose as if she smelled a three-day-old fish (unrefrigerated), and then strutted across the room to the sound of trumpets that only she could hear. (In her little pink flats that matched her little pink sweater—and in the days

that followed, it was blue and blue, yellow and yellow
. . . She was definitely color-coordinated.)

Now, at H.H. we mostly *like* getting a new kid. I mean,
it breaks up the routine (especially in January), and what
usually happens is that after the first couple of days, when
we find out the important stuff (age? boyfriend? favorite
rock group? and are her parents apt to let her have a party
without wandering through the room every five minutes?), she just settles in and becomes one of the crowd—
like Cissy or Mary Jo or Winkle Shultz.

But not Natalie Gatling.

I could tell that right away, or at least by lunchtime
when Janet Preller brought her along to the cafeteria and
she kept looking around and saying "pathetic." Now, the
cafeteria at Hawthorne Hills is pretty basic, what with
lots of noise and music and kids running around or sitting
on radiators and windowsills and everything smelling of
soybean burgers—but it's not exactly pathetic.

And to make it even worse, she (Natalie) sat there
explaining to everyone how her family moved here from
out of town in December, and how all the "good" private
schools were full and her mother finally managed to get
her into Hawthorne Hills. Then she laughed and did an
imitation of her mother telling Birdy-Morrison how *committed* she was to alternative schooling.

"When everybody knows it's bilge," said Natalie Gatling, dabbing her little pink mouth with her little pink
handkerchief.

And the thing was that all of a sudden I felt sorry for Birdy-Morrison, who believes (or wants to believe) everybody. It was sort of like having someone make fun of a favorite rag doll you'd had forever. And, for the first time, I began to see how Mrs. Hubbard felt about Dimples. (But if anything happened to Birdy-Morrison, I don't think I'd bother to replace her, much less pretend I hadn't.)

As if all this wasn't bad enough, when we got to creative writing that afternoon, there *she* was (Natalie Gatling, not Birdy-Morrison *or* Mrs. Hubbard), and when Sam asked her who she was, she told him in this voice that positively simpered, and right away he said "Gatling" was the name of a kind of gun. Which seemed appropriate.

But meanwhile my thoughts were spinning ahead.

Natalie Gatling.

Nat the Gat.

Gnat the Gat.

Gnat the Gnasty.

Gnaturally Gnasty.

Gnat the Gnaturally Gnasty Gat.

And by the time, in the interest of simplicity, I'd arrived back at Nat the Gat, I had missed great chunks of what was going on in class and for some reason everyone was talking about music. If you ask me, Nat the Gat is the type who gives classical music a bad name. I mean, there she was blathering on about "the three Bs—Bach, Beethoven, and Brahms" and how their kind of music was the *only* way to go.

"How about the *four* Bs—the Boomerangs?" I said.

And for a minute she looked as though maybe she was going to throw up. Then she said, "Oh, *you're* the girl who thinks her father is a Boomerang. I recognize you from your picture."

"I don't *think*—" I said.

"Obviously," said Nat the Gat.

Even before I had a chance to say "I *know*."

Sam must've (or might've, it's hard to tell what's intentional with Sam Klemkoski) felt the vibes in the room, because all of a sudden he changed the subject and gave us our next assignment (and three days to do it in!), which he introduced by saying, "So far this year we've concentrated on writing positively; now I think it's time you all had a chance to vent your spleens."

Vent your spleens?

But, like all teachers, he couldn't just *give* the assignment, he had to *talk* it to death first. All about idioms and what they said and what they meant and what did we think he meant by "venting your spleen."

"Windows in your intestines?" said Cissy. And Sam said that wasn't bad, since what it had to do with was letting out one's angry feelings. Then he gave a few sample titles: "I Get Mad Whenever I . . ." or "When My

Father Came Home and Said We Were Moving to Kansas
and I'd Never See My Best Friends Again, I Wanted to
. . ." or "The Most Reprehensible Character I Have
Known."

Ha!

The Most Reprehensible
Character I Have Known

*Without naming any names, I want to talk about the
most reprehensible character I have met—who (whom?)
I just did (meet) and who will hereafter be called R.C.
(reprehensible character), because I wouldn't want to
damage anyone's reputation, particularly someone's I
haven't known very long.*

But some things you know right away.

*I don't want to appear shallow, or like the kind of person
who judges a book by its cover or a girl by matching
shoes, sweaters, handkerchiefs, and probably underwear
(the kind that, I'll bet, says Monday, Tuesday, Wednesday, etc., along the side in squiggly letters). However, I
am very suspicious of a person who obviously doesn't own
any Reeboks or Adidas or even the imitation kind (the
ones that mothers are always telling you to get even as
they swear that no one will know the difference—which,
of course, they do). I am suspicious of someone who
carries her books in a tote bag that says* HEAVY READING
on the side, her lunch in paper bags that match what she

is wearing that day, and her head as though it might roll off her shoulders and break. And who probably, in the privacy of her own home, lounges around looking like a model from Seventeen *as she nibbles the end of her pencil and works on a list of "Twenty Things That Make Me Blush."*

Now, basically I believe in a person doing her own thing, except that at Hawthorne Hills everybody's own thing is pretty much the same, which is why I have trouble with somebody who wears stockings instead of big chunky socks and who talks in a little fluty voice, even when she says things that'll make your hair stand on end. That, and the fact that on her first day at Hawthorne Hills, R.C. (after saying that she recognized me in that sumo-wrestler picture that was in the paper) had the nerve to say the Boomerangs had always been "grossly overrated" and why would I want one of them for a father, anyway. Forcing me to defend them.

Even though I think someone should basically be her-self, sometimes I don't like it when she is—and that makes me feel contradictory. And sort of like an oxymoron.

As I may or may not have mentioned, R.C. is color-coordinated, which, all along, has led me to believe that she is the kind of daughter that Porter Martin's mother should have. When I described her to Porter and asked him what kind of sister he thought she'd be, he said, "A creep smeep." Then, because I still find myself intensely interested in Porter Martin's Boomerang-freak brother,

Wally (who hadn't come home for Christmas vacation either, because the entire family went to Aspen), I asked Porter what Wally would think. This time he didn't say anything; he just made barfing noises.

Notes from Sam Klemkoski to Sydney Downie: (1) Whom. (2) *The next-to-the-last paragraph doesn't quite work. An oxymoron is a figure of speech, not a person, and means the bringing together of contradictory terms, i.e., sweet sorrow or wise fool.* (3) Well, you <u>did</u> the assignment, which basically was to unload. Now, let's go on from there.

Which I assumed meant, give R.C. (aka Nat the Gat) a chance. Which will be hard to do.

There was something that, maybe as a result of my "Most Reprehensible Character" piece, was sort of weird, though. Lately Mrs. Hubbard had been getting on my case a lot—thumping on the floor (her ceiling) if I even played the stereo just loud enough to barely *hear* it; flopping around with her birds so early on weekend mornings that I had to put a pillow over my head to get any sleep at all; and sending me to the store to get cat food for Dimples (which was okay), but then making me go all the way back and exchange it (which was not okay), because (this) Dimples doesn't like canned food. I mean, how am I supposed to keep track of what her cat/cats eats/eat? Anyway, while I was in the venting-my-spleen mood and obviously on a roll, I thought I should just go on and deal with Mrs. Hubbard. Except that when I actually tried writing it all down, I found that venting one's spleen takes a lot of energy, which, it being January and all, I just didn't have.

(A digression, but if there's one thing I can't stand about my mother it's that any time I have a legitimate gripe— like Mrs. Hubbard, or the lowlife at the shoe store who sold me a pair of boots with one size six and one size seven and then got mad when I took them back—she's forever telling me to "be nice." Which may be her style, but definitely isn't mine.)

It's just as well that I didn't get involved in another angry piece, though, because about that time Sam told us to start thinking about a short story, and sometimes "thinking" about something takes more time than actually *doing* it. Anyway, a short story! A real one! I mean, I'd been writing short stories (or the beginnings of short stories) for ages, but just having Sam ask made it seem realer.

We were sitting in class and Sam was pacing up and down the room (which is not an easy thing to do, because at H.H. we sit all helter-skelter and not in rows) the day he told us about the story.

"We're going to try something a little more ambitious now," he said. "We're going to try a short story."

Everybody gasped and sat up straight.

"What I want you to do is to write a story, using as your protagonist your mother as a young girl," he said.

Everybody groaned.

"And in order to get a feel for your main character, make good use of the similarities between you and your mother: the way you sometimes hear *her* voice in *your* voice, find your reactions in hers."

Everybody said, "No way."

Sam turned to face us, shrugging his shoulders and throwing his hands up in the air as he said, " 'Plus ça change, plus c'est la même chose.' Does anyone know what that means?"

And he positively beamed at Nat the Gat when she said, in that revolting voice of hers, " 'The more things change, the more they stay the same.' "

I hate Natalie Gatling.

(And sometimes Sam Klemkoski.)

February

Mom and I celebrated Groundhog Day at Sam's, only *this* time Mom opened the door with a key, threw some wood in the stove, and told me that the place would warm up soon, so to take my coat off and stay awhile. And for some reason, having Mom seem to belong made me feel more like a stranger than I had the first time (when I *was* sort of a stranger). I mean, there she was, "at home" in Sam Klemkoski's house. Then I began to wonder how much "at home," and did I really want to know? But I guess I did, because I said I had to go to the bathroom and headed up the stairs. And up. First I got to this kind of balcony, which I guess had something to do with when the house was a bakery, and then on to the second floor, where there were two bathrooms—one with a tub (a whole room for just a tub?), one with a sink and toilet—both at subzero temperatures.

Just as I was about to go in (the one with the toilet), I was suddenly half afraid I'd find Mom's toothbrush, or a nightgown on the back of the door (the way the heroine's is in old movies). I didn't. I knew I shouldn't, but I went on to explore Sam's bedroom, which was in the front of the house and was big and spare-looking and empty except for a bed, a dresser, and an enormous mural that took up one whole wall. And a stack of books by the side of the bed. I stared at the mural and thought how I liked it, even if it was weird-looking, and wished I could ask Sam about it, except that I couldn't because how was I going to explain being in his room in the first place?

I looked over the room again, mentally storing up things to tell Cissy and Mary Jo about it, until I realized that I'd never even told them anything *about* Mom and Sam (whatever there was *to* tell). I had told Porter, though, and he said that if Mom married Sam Klemkoski, then we wouldn't have to live with Mrs. Hubbard anymore, which was something I hadn't thought about (Mom marrying S.K., that is—I think about not having to live with Mrs. Hubbard all the time). But then Porter said, "Unless she made arrangements for just *you* to stay with Mrs. Hubbard, anyway." Which, of course, *my* mother would never do but Porter's mother *might*. And it made me sad that he would think that way.

*   *   *

Note from Sydney Downie to Sydney Downie: *Remember to remove this section the next time S.K. collects the journals. (Whoever thought mine would have to be censored—and all because of my mother?)*

I heard the front door slam and flew down the steps, trying to look innocent and as if I'd really just been going to the bathroom. I needn't have bothered, though, because when I got to the studio, my mother and Sam Klemkoski were just standing there giving each other these disgusting gloppy looks, and I could swear he had his arm around her, except that right away he started unloading about a million boxes of Chinese food. Sometimes I wish Sam's taste would become a little more eclectic (that's a word he's been pushing a lot lately and it means, roughly, liking a bunch of different things).

And I wish he'd leave my mother alone. At least I *think* I do.

Anyway, we ate, and Mom and Sam talked, and I felt dumb and in the way and wished I hadn't come. Finally, I picked up a magazine and went and sat over in the corner, half reading it and half looking at the chunk of wood in the middle of the studio which was suddenly a lot more interesting than it'd been before. I mean, now there were bits and shavings of wood on the floor all around it, and the thing itself was beginning to have a shape. I wasn't sure what *kind* of shape, because it was big and rough and raw-looking, but it *was* a shape.

After a while, even an emerging shape starts to get boring, though, and I began to twist around in my chair, scuff my feet, and get that really rotten feeling you get when you know you're being really rotten. I kept sighing and saying how I had to get home and do my homework, until Mom finally got up and grabbed her coat and said, "Come on, then." The awful part was, that made me feel exactly the way I used to when I was little and Mom and I were out someplace and I had to go to the bathroom and she'd say, "Why didn't you go before we left the house?" (Which I always had.)

Besides, how was I supposed to know she was going to want to spend the entire evening? And why didn't Sam get back to work? On the way home I told my mother that we should've left sooner because now Sam would have to stay up all night working and then he'd be really grouchy and zombielike the next day. Mom didn't say anything; she just pressed down harder on the accelerator.

And the next day Sam was—grouchy and zombielike.

Which is why he let us write during class time (a variation on the old taking-the-class-to-the-library routine) while he sat with his head in his hands, fighting sleep.

Short Story
How Martha Met the Boomerangs

It was a dark and stormy night . . .

It was a bright and shiny morning . . .

The sun was shining brightly when Martha Foley opened the door and . . .

The fog was so thick that the pretty American girl could hardly see her hand in front of her face . . .

Maybe I should just forget the weather. I mean, who really *cares* if the sun was shining, or if Martha could see her hand in front of her face. I put my pencil down and bent my fingers backward, one at a time, until they cracked, and Sam groaned. Next to me, Cissy was erasing something and blowing on the page, then hunching over to write again before she repeated the whole process: erasing, blowing, writing; erasing, blowing, writing. On the other side, Mary Jo sat staring into space. I could understand where both of them were coming from.

But not Nat the Gat. *She* was across the room writing furiously and setting up a gale the way she was turning pages, though it's hard to understand how she could actually see with all that long black hair falling into her face. For a minute I thought it was an act: that she was really writing out a bunch of nursery rhymes or a letter to a friend—just to unnerve the rest of us. But then I remembered that grossly disgusting remark she made at lunch the other day about how when she writes, the "words flow like jewels" from her pen.

Arrrgh! Jewels? Pebbles would be more like it. I closed my eyes and saw Nat the Gat leaving a trail of pebbles (the kind you see in fishbowls) all across her paper. Then I remembered the time there was a mouse in Mrs. Hubbard's kitchen (briefly, thanks to Dimples) and it left a trail of something else in the silverware drawer. Which I hoped was a lot more like what N. the G. was writing. Then I had this hideous thought that maybe she was actually *good*, which I could tell right away was going to take up a lot of my worrying time in the weeks ahead.

I've been worrying a lot lately. I read somewhere that if you have a bunch of things to worry about, it's a good idea to set aside a special "worrying time" every day and devote half an hour to it and no more. That way, according to the article, you can then "get on with your life." The trouble is that if I now have to add whether Nat the Gat's words really "flow like jewels" from her pen, it's possible I could use up too much of my allotted time with just that. Then what would I do with all the other stuff: what's happening with my mother and Sam K.; nuclear holocaust; Mrs. Hubbard and how Mom and I should get a place of our own; acid rain; why Porter Martin's mother doesn't pay more attention to him and am I ever going to meet Wally; my Boomerang blood and what, if anything, I can do to get my mother and

Jamie back together (because, the way I see it, even an *ex*-Boomerang'd be better than a sculptor/English teacher). (I think.)

At this point Sam groaned again and said, "Some of you don't seem to be *writing* anything," which I thought was an unfair remark, since Sam Klemkoski, of all people, ought to understand about the thinking part. Writing a short story is hard work (at least for me it is). The trouble is that I never know how to make things happen or even (and I think as a would-be writer I shouldn't admit this) *what* to make happen. I mean, there it is, a rainy day in Australia (Where in Australia? I can hear Sam say in my head). And there's Martha, and there's Jamie. But how do they meet? And did they, really? Which was such a disturbing thought that I squashed it into the back of my head and started to write.

Short Story
How Martha Met the Boomerangs

It was a rainy day in Sydney and a young American girl named Martha Foley was walking along the street, minding her own business and thinking about the courses she was taking at school. In fact, Martha was so preoccupied that she wasn't paying any attention to where she was going, and it probably wouldn't have meant anything to her, anyway. Besides that, she had always been a serious girl, with straight brown hair and glasses. The rain was stinging her face as she went past a building with a lot of people hanging around out front. In fact, I think they were the "Boomerettes" and the place was the Ayers recording studio. Just then, the door opened and a tall thin man with streaky brown hair that was short on the sides and long in back (with spiky bangs) came out, and all of a sudden the Boomerettes were pushing and shoving and Martha ended up in the street. The tall thin man whipped off his shirt and threw it down so Martha could get back onto the curb without getting her feet any wetter. And it was just like Sir Walter Raleigh and Queen Elizabeth. Except that the man was Jamie Ward the Boomerang and the woman was a young unknown girl from the States.

I sat back and sighed and thought how, for once, the words had sort of flowed from my pen, even though I was pretty sure they weren't like jewels, and if they were I'd cut out my tongue rather than mention it, because that's the kind of thing that makes people hate you (and I liked to think it was the difference between me and Nat the Gat). At the end of class Sam collected our papers, which I thought was sort of unfair because what if some of us were really on a roll and just wanted to keep going (and from the look of Sam, he wasn't going to read those papers, anyway).

That afternoon, when school was over and we were all hanging out in the Big Hall, Nat the Gat came up to where a bunch of us were sitting and just stood there, tapping one little yellow shoe. "Well, Sydney," she said when everybody had stopped talking and was looking at her, "I saw your mother with Sam Klemkoski the other day and they were so busy with what they were doing they didn't even notice me. Even when I said hello."

What were they doing? I wanted to ask, but didn't. Winkle Shultz did, though, and Nat the Gat just rolled her eyes and said, "Oh, *you* know."

Which I didn't.

It turns out that N. the G. had seen Mom and Sam in the museum on Sunday (and what can you *do* in a museum, anyway?).

Then she made this big thing about how she wondered if Birdy-Morrison knew there was *fraternization* taking place on her faculty. And the way she said "fraternization" it sounded like a dirty word.

"My mother's never spent a night out in her entire life," I said, realizing as soon as the words were out of my mouth that she really hadn't, and since that was the case why had I bothered checking Sam's upstairs? Then I remembered this movie Cissy and Mary Jo and I'd seen on cable once where they (the hero and heroine) did it in the middle of the afternoon. In broad daylight.

Just when I was beginning to worry about that, I heard Nat the Gat saying, "Well, she will. Just give her time."

"She will not," I shouted. "Anyway, my mother'd never do anything to besmirch my father's memory."

"Whatever you say, Boomerang brain," said Nat the Gat.

And what's really the pits was that everybody laughed.

And even worse, I'd expected Cissy and Mary Jo to take my side, or at least sympathize, and they didn't. In fact, they both just got really mad that I hadn't told them my mother was dating Sam Klemkoski.

Which I never thought of her as doing. I mean, *dating* sounds pretty gross for a middle-aged woman.

It turned out that Sam *did* read the papers we turned in, but when I got to creative writing early the next day and he started in on mine, I wished he hadn't. I mean, he said that even though Australia was a friendly place, did I really think my mother would've been wandering the streets of Sydney talking to strangers? "It seems out of character," he said.

"It's fiction," I said. "I thought we were writing *stories.*"

"Yes," said Sam. "But how about the demands of veri-similitude?" Which I think has something to do with truth.

After that, Sam went all around the room doing the same kind of nit-picking. And all around the room you could hear people saying, "But it's just a *story.*" Finally Sam started pulling on his ear and running his fingers through his hair and looking the way he'd looked at the beginning of the year (his greased-pig look), and then he said, "Well, maybe having you use your mothers as your main characters wasn't a very good idea. Go ahead and change them if you want. Give them new names, new backgrounds, new personalities."

But the thing was, I knew I couldn't do that. I mean, this was Martha's story. And Jamie's. And mine (eventually).

Sam gave the papers back, and when he handed me mine he said to go on with it but that I'd better do something about the title—that I'd already told "How Martha Met the Boomerangs" and it was only the first paragraph.

Well, some things are easy to fix. Right across the top of my paper I wrote the new title—*Jamie and Martha: Destiny*.

Sam spent the whole rest of the class reading just the beginnings of other people's stories (real writers', I mean) out loud so we'd know what we were supposed to do. But after a while they all blurred together and I had to keep pinching myself to stay awake. And I decided that maybe I'd better give my story a rest and catch up on my geometry.

Interesting (and unsettling) question: That night, I was telling my mother about Sam getting rattled in class (I *didn't* tell her about the Jamie and Martha story) and I said, "He always used to twiddle his toes when he got upset."

And my mother said, "He still does."

How does she know that?

"How do you know *that*?" I screeched. "I mean, there's about a ton of snow out there."

"That's how I know," my mother said. "When we got back to his place after the museum the other day, Sam's shoes were wet and he took them off and walked around in his bare feet."

Yeah. Tell me about it. I mean, in *that* house, with no central heating? Anyway, I must've been looking at Mom kind of funny because all of a sudden she turned pink and said, "Oh, for heaven's sake, Sydney," and left the room.

Sometimes mothers can be *so* condescending.

But when my mother is being condescending, at least she's being condescending *to* someone (me), and if you ask me, that's a lot better than being uninterested *in*. Which is exactly what Porter Martin's mother sometimes is. (And the reason I know it's *un*interested and not *dis*interested is that Sam makes a big thing of that—how *dis* means impartial and *un* means sort of actively not interested.) I mean, *my* mother'd never have done what Porter's mother did with the bird feeder.

Now, if you ask me, it shouldn't matter that the bird feeder was spindly and wobbly, with nails sticking out of the top. Or that Porter'd forgotten to leave a place for the food to go. I mean, he made it, didn't he? And brought it home and put it right on the kitchen table, where it stayed until the next day, when he found it in the garbage can, along with an empty cereal box and a grapefruit rind. The really sad part is that when he told me about it, I got mad and Porter didn't. All he said was "It's okay, Sydney. Okay smokay."

What I wished I could've done then was get hold of Mrs. Martin and send her "Out to the Outback" (as in the Boomerangs' song), which seemed to me to be a very good place for her.

Valentine's Day came and went, and I was doing a pretty good job of not asking my mother where the dozen long-stemmed red roses she brought home from school had come from. And she was doing a good job of not telling me. In fact, we could've maintained what I think is called the status quo if it hadn't been for Nat the Gat.

"Well, I guess Sam Klemkoski gave your mother all those roses I saw her with yesterday. It's hard to imagine how he could've afforded them on what he must make teaching at a school like this," she said the next morning. And my two former best friends, Cissy and Mary Jo, laughed and bobbed their heads up and down like puppets on a string. Their laughter was *at* me rather than *with* me, so that for a minute I felt the way I had in grade school the time Janet Preller threw a dodgeball and hit me in the stomach and I just stood there and couldn't breathe.

But this time I recovered quickly. "Why don't you go someplace *else*, then?" I asked.

"Slumming is good for the soul," said Nat the Gat. And behind her, Cissy and Mary Jo made mindless hee-hee-hee noises, and for the first time I noticed that instead of Reeboks and leg warmers they had on matching little red flats (matching N. the G.'s, I mean).

" 'One man's meat is another man's poison,' " I said, not sure that was really what I meant, but I *had* to say something.

"You have to admit it's run-down," said Mary Jo.

"And that it *should* be co-ed," said Cissy.

"And the facilities are *pitiful*," said Natalie Gatling.

For a minute I wanted to remind Cissy and Mary Jo that one of the things we'd always loved about Hawthorne Hills was that it was sort of run-down, and lived-in, and comfortable, and not like all those homogenized schools that look the same and where the classrooms sometimes don't even have windows. That, and the fact that with Milton High just down the street, there're plenty of guys around—without our actually having to go to school with them, *or* having them see us in our gym suits. (And given the way I look in my gym suit, that's a distinct advantage.)

But instead of saying any of that, I decided to stand on my dignity (as Mrs. Hubbard sometimes says), turned on my heel (hard to do in a Reebok), and walked away, vowing once and for all to devote myself almost exclusively to my writing.

Short Story
Jamie and Martha: Destiny
(paragraph 2)

After Jamie helped Martha back up onto the curb, he picked up his shirt and brushed it off. When he put it back on, he was really wet and shivering, so Martha said to come along and have a cup of tea and that she'd pay.

Dumb. Martha wouldn't've said that. Not the part about paying, anyway, though she probably would've felt in her purse to see if she had enough money just in case they went for tea and Jamie didn't pay. I mean, that's what I did the time I was in the mall and ran into Bobby Miller and he said, "Come on, let's get a soda." Which I thought was maybe what Sam Klemkoski meant when he talked about the similarities between us and our mothers. I crossed out what I'd written and began again.

Jamie and Martha: Destiny
(paragraph 2)

The Boomerettes were still pushing and pulling as Jamie Ward reached for his shirt with one hand and for Martha Foley with the other. "Come on, and we'll have a cup of tea," he said. "But I don't know you," she said. "You're kidding?" he said, looking really surprised. "That's very refreshing. Come along, and we'll have two cups of tea. Two each, I mean."

I have just decided that writing dialogue is the hardest thing in the world. I mean, I never in my life heard anyone say, "That's very refreshing" (except, once, Mrs. Hubbard, and she was talking about iced tea with mint in it). I put my head down in my hands and tried to think what Jamie would've said to Martha. What my father would've said to my mother.

Jamie and Martha: Destiny
(paragraph 2)

"Hi," said the young man with the brown hair as he reached down for the girl in the puddle of rain. "My name is Jamie." "My name is Martha," the girl said as she got up, brushed herself off, and handed him his shirt. "Jamie Ward," he said. "Martha Foley," she said. And right at that moment he realized that she was probably the only person left in Sydney who didn't know who he was, and he found that very refreshing. "Let's have a cup of tea," he said. "Okay," she said, so bedazzled by his piercing eyes that she didn't even bother to look in her purse to see if she had enough money.

At this point I decided that maybe what I should do was give up short-story writing—at least till I could figure out how to make my characters talk without sounding moronic. Everybody must've been having the same kind of trouble because when we got to class the next day Sam said, "Let's not bother with those stories today." Then he took a piece of chalk and wrote on the board: *"I'd Like to Be Stranded on a Desert Island with . . ."* or *"But on Second Thought . . ."* and said to choose one.

After that, he went and settled into a chair in the corner and sat brooding over his hands, and I could tell just by looking at him that he'd had a hard night with the block of wood.

The trouble was that there was *no one* I wanted to be stranded on a desert island with right about then, which was a very lonely thing for a person to have to say about herself. And as for the other topic—"But on Second Thought . . ."—I didn't even know what that meant.

Then all of a sudden I did, and it was as if a bolt of lightning had flashed in my head, and I knew what I was going to write and how I was going to combine both topics into one piece.

Two for the Price of One
(as Mrs. Hubbard sometimes says)

I'd like to be stranded on a desert island with Cissy, because for as far back as I can remember, Cissy and I have been best friends. In fact, I don't even remember meeting *Cissy, she's just always been there, the way my mother and Mrs. Hubbard were always there. The thing about Cissy and me is that we always know what the other one is thinking and half the time don't have to* say *anything, which is a good thing to be able to say about* *someone to be stranded on a desert island <u>with</u>. Even after we started school (Hawthorne Hills, because my mother taught there and got my tuition free, and also because she <u>believed</u> in it) and met Mary Jo and she became the third part of our triumvirate, Cissy was always very special to me.*

But, on second thought, things are different now. And all because of a certain person who shall remain nameless but whose initials are N.G. or N. the G. It's just that I expect friends to be loyal and keep things the way they've always been, and to stick up for me, which Cissy is definitely not doing. In fact, she doesn't even <u>look</u> like Cissy anymore, and yesterday when she told me to get my "Boomerang bones" out of the way, she didn't <u>sound</u> like Cissy but like the aforementioned someone.

Right now I feel bruised and raw and like I have a toothache all over. And I would expect a real friend to understand about my mother and Jamie and what it's like to have a famous father.

In the words of Jamie Ward and the other three Boomerangs: "Save Me!"

Note from Sam Klemkoski to Sydney Downie: *In the further words of the Boomers: "Time to Let It Go," Sydney.*
Which was no help at all.

We celebrated Washington's Birthday at Sam's studio (it's really called Presidents' Day now, but Sam says, to a purist, it'll always be Washington's Birthday). He made a cherry pie, which we ate after the boxes of Chinese food (my mother's contribution, so maybe what they have is a sentimental attachment to Chinese food).

Later, when we'd finished eating, I wandered over to the big piece of wood in the center of the room, except that by this time it was definitely more than a piece of wood. Now it seemed to have a life of its own and a sort of great strength. I still didn't know what it was supposed to be and was beginning to think that maybe I never would and that that would be all right, too. I put my hand on it and was just standing there when S.K. came up to me.

"I think I owe you an apology, Sydney," he said. "I'm afraid my note after your last piece was too flip—that I sacrificed substance for the bon mot."

I didn't know what a bon mot was. Besides that, it was really weird—having Sam apologize—so right away I sort of had to hang tough and tell him that I hadn't meant any of it: that I'd just wanted to get something down on paper.

"Okay, but just remember I'm here, and I know about those all-over toothaches."

On the way home in the car, while my mother was singing along with the radio (which I swear, in all the years I've known her, she's never done), I thought about how I was feeling good and that maybe it was because of Sam and what he'd said.

March

"How's the Boomerang brat this morning?" said Nat the Gat, blowing into the Big Hall. And the thing was that she was literally blowing in (or being blown), because it was March and this year March'd definitely come in like a lion.

"Heard from your famous father lately?" said Nat the Gat. "You *do* hear from him?" she went on, pecking away like a woodpecker on a tree, while all I was doing was trying to figure out a way not to lie without actually telling the truth.

"You *do* keep up your end of the correspondence, I hope. I mean, the world still needs the fine art of letter writing, don't you agree?" said Nat the Gat, turning to her clones Cissy and Mary Jo, who bobbed their heads up and down.

"Yeah, well, I owe him a letter, sort of," I said, feeling all of a sudden that I'd stepped into a trap.

And when I walked into creative writing later that day and saw that Sam Klemkoski had written THE FINE ART OF LETTER WRITING on the board, all in capital letters, I heard that trap snap shut behind me.

"How long has it been since any of you wrote a letter?" he asked when everybody'd settled down.

"Last week, when I sent a snapshot of my boyfriend away to be made into a giant poster," said Janet Preller.

"A *real* letter," said Sam.

"I wrote to a school in Pennsylvania once to find out about being a veterinary assistant," said Mary Jo.

"And in it you said?" Sam waited.

"Nothing, really. It was a coupon. The kind they have in the backs of magazines."

"Exactly," said Sam, changing what was on the board to THE LOST ART OF LETTER WRITING.

"Except that it doesn't matter anymore, because I think I'd rather be a flight attendant," said Mary Jo, more to herself than to anyone else.

"Anyway, we *did* letters, way back before Christmas," I said, wondering how Sam could've forgotten that it was because of my letter getting in the paper and winning the prize that I'd brought *my* mother to *his* studio, which I guess was the beginning of the relationship they have now.

But just then I heard Sam come out with a loud "Aha," and for a minute I thought he was going to write that on the board, too. (And for a minute I could almost see it there, all in capitals. AHA.)

"In those letters we espoused causes," said Sam. "We expressed our opinions, we relayed information. In short, we wrote letters to the editor. What I'm talking about now is the social letter, which seems close on the heels of the dodo bird, as it wends its way into extinction."

Dodo bird? Wends its way? I wrote on a piece of paper; but just as I started to show it to Cissy, I remembered that we didn't do that kind of thing anymore and balled it up in the palm of my hand.

"This is an instant society we live in," said Sam, sitting on the windowsill in such a way that the sunlight made the hair in his ears look like Brillo pads. "Instant mashed potatoes, instant oatmeal, instant communication—with AT&T urging us to 'reach out and touch someone.' Instantly, by pressing a button, not even taking the time to *dial* anymore. When was the last time any of you *got* a letter?"

"I got one from the poster company, telling me to send more money," said Janet Preller.

"A *real* letter," said Sam. "The kind you settle down at the kitchen table to read, not even caring that your coffee's getting cold or the toast is burning."

And when nobody said anything, he just sat there for a minute, shaking his head. "Where would the world be without the great letter writers?" he said after a while. "Without Lord Byron, Jane and Thomas Carlyle, Robert Louis Stevenson? Without the letters Vincent van Gogh wrote to his brother, Theo? What do any of you know about letters like that?"

"They're worth a lot of money," said Nat the Gat.

"Money?" said Sam, in a voice that sounded like air going out of a tire. "Well, I guess."

More head shaking, until he finally said, "Who are *you* going to write to? And don't tell me about poster companies or schools for veterinary assistants. Who? Who? Who?"

"Who?" he said again, this time jabbing his finger into the air.

"Maybe my aunt," said Winkle Shultz. "I mean, I have to thank her for a birthday present, anyway, so I guess I could write instead of calling."

"Who?"

"I had a pen pal once in fourth grade, but I think she's moved," said Brenda Patch.

"Who?" said Sam.

"Ask Sydney Downie, why don't you," said Nat the Gat. "She has someone to write to. She was bragging about it just this morning, in the Big Hall."

"Who, Sydney?" said Sam, coming to stand in front of me with that look of hope teachers get on their faces when they think somebody's *finally* going to come up with the right answer.

Except that I didn't.

"Who?" said Janet Preller.

"Who?"

"Who?"

"Who?" said Cissy, Winkle, and Mary Jo.

The word bounced around me like a Ping-Pong ball, and I put up my hands to bat it away.

"Who?" said Nat the Gat.

"My father," I shouted. "I said I owed a letter to my father."

"Oh," said Sam, into the silence that followed.

"And then," said Natalie Gatling, after a while, "she can bring the answer in to show the rest of us. A *real* letter from a *real* Boomerang. She could even *sell* it. And make a lot of money."

I slouched down lower in my chair and thought how if I ever did get a letter from Jamie Ward I'd never in a million years *sell* it. Unless, of course, it was to get money so that Mom and I could move into our own place and not have to live with Mrs. Hubbard anymore. Though I was pretty sure that even a Boomerang letter wouldn't pay for an apartment. And then I began to feel sort of guilty, even to think of selling a letter from my father (which, of course, he hadn't written).

For the rest of the period Sam read letters written by

famous people (Lord Byron, Jane and Thomas Carlyle, Robert Louis Stevenson), but I didn't pay much attention and when class was over I just sat in the empty classroom, wondering how it could be that I'd come in feeling okay and was going out feeling so sort of trampled.

Cissy was waiting for me in the hall, and right away she started talking in this one long sentence, as though she was afraid that if she didn't get it all out at once, she wouldn't get it out at all. "Listen, Sydney, I mean, this morning when Natalie was coming into school she heard Sam telling your mother how he was tired from being up late working and how he hadn't had time to prepare and on account of that he was going to have us write letters because it was easy—for him, anyway—and the thing is he just kept going on about 'the fine art of letter writing.'

"And that's why she did it to you. Natalie. Why she set you up, I mean." Cissy stopped and took a deep breath.

And for a minute it was just the way it used to be. Me and Cissy together, with one of us telling the other something incredibly important. In fact, it was *so much* like it used to be that I was all set to ask if she wanted to go somewhere for a piece of pizza after school, except that all of a sudden she said she had to go, and took off down the hall. And the bizarre thing was, I had this feeling that if I dashed downstairs I'd find Nat the Gat at the other end of an invisible string, pulling Cissy in faster and faster.

When I got home, the house was empty. It may sound weird, but I can tell, just by walking in the door, whether a house is *really* empty (the same way I can tell, when I call someone on the telephone, if there's anyone there to hear it ringing). Anyway, the house was empty (except for Dimples), so I made a peanut-butter sandwich and took it upstairs. The whole time I was eating it I was thinking about Sam and "the fine art of letter writing" and why I hadn't ever written to Jamie and if I should now, and if I did, what could I say. After a while I got out a piece of paper and right away I discovered one of the reasons I'd never written to him before. I didn't even know how to *start*.

Dear Jamie . . . I couldn't say that. I mean, that's what I call him to myself, but I've never actually *met* him (unless I did when I was a baby, which I don't remember and which wouldn't count—at least not for letter-writing purposes).

Dear Mr. Ward . . . To my father?

Dear Dad . . . Which totally freaked me out and made me tear the paper to shreds.

✳   ✳   ✳

Then I decided that maybe to start out I shouldn't write to Jamie at all, but to his mother, my grandmother, instead. In one of Wally Martin's books I'd read that after the Boomerangs got famous, Jamie's mother spent a lot of time answering fan letters, and I figured that even though this wasn't exactly a *fan* letter, she'd probably be glad to answer mine. If she was still alive. And the thought that she might not be made me feel sad. But let's face it, if Jamie was born in 1947 and was the youngest in his family, that could make his mother pretty old by now. Except that I suddenly remembered Katharine Hepburn and Mother Teresa and decided that Jamie's mother was probably no older than them. I hoped.

Dear Margaret . . . Well, if I couldn't say "Dear Jamie," I certainly couldn't say "Dear Margaret . . ."

Dear Mrs. Ward . . . To my grandmother?

Dear Granny . . . No way.

I was just tearing up *that* piece of paper when the phone rang. It was Mrs. Martin, wanting to know if I would take Porter to a play he was in at school tonight; she'd drive us there, but then she had to go look at curtain material, and Mr. Martin had a meeting, but he'd bring us home, and all that really mattered was that Porter have a warm body in the audience. That's what she said. A warm body. Yuck.

I said I'd do it, and then went downstairs to make tuna-fish salad so we could eat as soon as Mom got home. (And figured that "the lost art of letter writing" could stay lost as far as I was concerned.)

Anyway, Mrs. Martin drove us there, and Porter was a goat in the play, and then afterward Mr. Martin picked us up and drove us home, and when he went to pay me I said no—that I didn't want money for going to see a friend in a play. Which made me sound either noble (which I'm not) or like what Mrs. Hubbard calls a Goody Two-shoes (which I'm not). It's just that as much as I want money, sometimes my principles are as strong as my greed.

By the time I got home I was really mad—it was one of those mad-at-everything feelings—and not at any one thing in particular. Except that I guess if I had to say, it would be at Mrs. Martin for going curtain shopping and at Mr. Martin for going to a meeting (which turned out to be *tennis*—I know because I almost sat on his tennis racquet, and also because of the way he smelled). And at Porter for being the best goat in the barnyard, with nobody (from his family) there to see him.

And there was nothing I could do about it.

Except that I did.

Letter-Writing Assignment

Dear Wally,

What kind of a brother are you, anyway? What kind of a brother cares more about going skiing and off with friends and even to camp (camp? at your age?) than spending <u>any time at all</u> home with his little brother, who just tonight was the <u>best</u> goat in the barnyard in his class play, with no one but a baby-sitter (me) there to watch (his particular goat didn't actually <u>say</u> anything), and who generally spends more time with me (the baby-sitter) and the housekeeper and even the plant waterer than with anyone in his very own family. And besides that, Porter is a neat kid (or, as he would say, neat smeat).

Sincerely,
Sydney Downie

P.S. Thanks for lending me your Boomerang books and records (which you may not know you <u>did</u> lend), but since you never come home I guess it's no big deal to you. But thanks, anyway.

P.P.S. And don't you think it's just the tiniest bit odd that the address inside your Boomerang books is your <u>school</u> address, and doesn't that say <u>something</u>?

P.P.P.S. One warm body is not as good as another.

When I went into creative writing the next day, I told Sam I'd already written my letter and mailed it. "To your . . . to Jamie Ward?" he said, and when I said no, he breathed a deep sigh. Then when I said I'd written to the brother of a friend, who was away at school, he got this sort of knowing look on his face and said "Aha" again and told me I could go to the library and continue working on my short story if I wanted.

Which is what I should've done. Except that for some reason I can't explain, I stopped at the pay phone and called the big downtown library and asked them if Jamie Ward the Boomerang's mother was still alive and did they know her address. It wasn't long before the voice came back on the phone and said that she was sorry but Margaret Ward had died of cancer in 1972 and was there anything else she could help me with.

I don't remember saying no, or thank you, or even hanging up. The next thing I knew, I was sitting in the school library feeling intensely sad and thinking how Margaret had died before I was born, which meant I never had a grandmother, or at least not a live one, and that all the time I'd been thinking about writing to her I couldn't've, anyway. Suddenly Maddie Stephens, the librarian, was hovering over me, saying "Sydney, what's wrong?"

"My grandmother died," I said, tears welling up in my eyes.

"Oh, you poor thing," she said, putting her arm around me and patting me on the shoulder.

Which is definitely more than my own mother did when she sent for me later in the day.

"What do you *mean* by telling Maddie Stephens your

grandmother died?" she said, her face looking danger-
ously spotted.

"Well, I called the—"

"Do you realize what an embarrassing position you put
me in?" my mother went on. "There was Maddie bringing
me a good strong cup of tea and asking me what I was
doing in school and what were the arrangements and had
my mother been ill long—and the next thing you know,
she'd've been taking up a collection from the other teachers for flowers. The only thing I could think to say to get
her off my back was that it was your *father's* mother,
which is patently ridiculous because your father's mother
died when Arthur was still a little boy, and I can't imagine
what I was thinking, and now you've made a more com-
plete fool out of me."

"But she did," I said.

"Who?"

"My grandmother."

"What?"

"Die," I said. "That's what I was trying to tell you.
That I called the library and they told me that Margaret
Ward died in 1972."

"Who's Margaret Ward?" my mother asked.

"Jamie's mother."

Then I had to help my mother into a chair, where she
sat for a long time, shaking her head and rocking back
and forth until she finally said, in a low, sort of strangled

voice, "Sydney Downie, I *never* want to hear any of this Boomerang blather again. Do you understand?"

For a minute I thought I should find Mom another cup of strong tea, but then I decided I should just get out of there. At least until Mom had a chance to pull herself together.

When I got back to the library, Maddie Stephens was poring over some big fat reference book. She looked up when I came in and said, "Oh, Sydney, it says here that Jamie Ward's mother . . ."

"Yeah, I know," I said. "In 1972. But sometimes, whenever I think of it, I feel really sad."

"I understand. And if you ever want to talk, you know where to find me."

"Yeah, thanks," I said, sniffling and making my way back to the far corner of the library.

Jamie and Martha: Destiny
(continued)

After Jamie and Martha had their tea, they went back to the Ayers studio and Jamie showed her around and introduced her to the other Boomerangs. For a while Martha was embarrassed because she didn't know who the Boomerangs were, but it didn't take long for her to find out, mainly because they all talked a lot. Pudge played the drums and Clive and Oscar were working on a song, and from time to time they'd stop and play what they had so far, then change it and play it again.

From that time on, Martha and Jamie spent almost every day together. They went to the Circular Quay and took a boat to the Taronga Zoo, where Martha had her picture taken in front of the kangaroo paddock. They walked through The Rocks and went on to Bennelong Point to see the Opera House. They ate carpetbag steak.

One day Jamie took Martha to Paddington (which he called Paddo) and showed her the house where he was born and also the Billabong Club. In turn, Martha took him through the University of Sydney and showed him where she went to class. The whole time they were walking around, Jamie had his hat pulled down over his face so nobody would recognize him. Which they didn't.

Later that day Jamie and Martha went out to the suburbs, where Jamie's parents lived in a lovely bungalow with a beautiful garden that their son had bought for them. When they got there, Margaret Ward was busy answering fan letters for her famous son, but she put them aside so she could fix tea for everyone. Jamie's mother made Martha Foley feel right at home, and when it was time to leave, she gave her half of a cake to take back to Sydney with her and told her to come again. On the way back, Martha kept thinking that Margaret Ward was just the kind of grandmother she'd want her child to have if she ever had one (a child).

I looked back over what I had written and realized that some of the "time" things were wrong. I mean, if my mother (Martha) had gone to see Margaret Ward in her bungalow in Appleton, and if Margaret had died in 1972, that would've put Mom in Australia sooner than I think she was. Then I remembered how one day in class Sam Klemkoski had talked about "your story taking on a life of its own."

Which I think is what mine just did.

Spring came to Hawthorne Hills, and the way we knew it was that Birdy-Morrison stood up in the Big Hall and gave her "Welcome, Springtime" talk (which is only slightly different from her "Goodbye, Girls" or her "Welcome Back, Girls" talks). In fact, it occurs to me that everything Birdy-Morrison says sounds pretty much the same. Which is all right, and sort of comfortable, and a little bit like it was when Mom used to read me "Yertle the Turtle" every night. Anyway, she (Birdy-M.) ended her springtime talk by saying, "And now, remember your self-awareness, girls." Which sent me off to the library to find Bartlett's *Familiar Quotations* and look up all those other "Remember" things ("the Alamo," "Lot's wife," "the Maine") that people are always talking about, and I wondered if years from now "Remember your self-awareness, girls" would be there, with Birdy-Morrison's name at the top of the page.

* * *

I could also tell it was spring because there were cro-
cuses poking up in the front yard, alongside the hedge.
And because Dimples was acting silly.

Almost as silly as my mother.

Now, the thing is that my mother, Martha Foley
Downie (Ward), is usually the most incredibly serious
person. I mean, we're talking deadpan here. But the
Saturday after Birdy-Morrison's speech, I came in from
the store and Sam Klemkoski and my mother were up in
our living room (which I may have mentioned is a converted porch) and they were laughing. Hysterically. And
the thing was that as soon as my mother saw me she
looked embarrassed, almost as if I'd caught her and Sam
making out. Her face kept twitching, and when I told
her that Mrs. Hubbard was standing at the bottom of the
steps, pretending to dust but I thought she was *listening*,
she cracked up again. Giggling, this time. And hiccuping.
With big fat tears rolling down her face.

When she'd finally gone into the bathroom to get a
drink of water, Sam wiped *his* eyes and said, "It's good
to see your mother laugh, Sydney. We'll have to get her
to do more of that." Then he went on about how hard
it'd been for my mother, a young widow with a baby.
And what she needed was a little *fun* in her life.

My mother?

At that point I figured I had two choices—to gag or to
leave—so I went down the stairs (past Mrs. Hubbard,

who'd moved up a step and was working away at the baseboard), outside, and through the hedge. Porter Martin was jumping on his trampoline. (Another sure sign of spring.)

"Jump smump," said Porter.

Which I did for a while, until I gave up and went to sit on the steps, watching Porter and thinking about a bunch of stuff. Like what it was like to see my mother *laughing out loud* and how weird it was to have a mother who looked weird laughing. (Which is not to say Mom's a grouch, because she's definitely not.) Then I worried a little about how maybe Mom was too serious for Sam Klemkoski and how he might not stick around. Which I suddenly found made me a little bit sad. (And it wasn't even my official worrying time.)

Then I cleared my mind and just sat there for a time, watching Porter. But one thing I've discovered: it's hard to keep your mind clear for very long. I mean, there I was, watching Porter, the way he jumped up and down. And all of a sudden I was thinking that the way Porter used the trampoline was the way Sam Klemkoski taught creative writing: bouncing from one thing to another—stories, essays, letters.

Which all seems pretty heavy for early spring.

On Monday morning Sam was into his trampoline mode. I mean, forget essays and letters. We were into dialogue.

"Who knows the difference between dialogue in real life and dialogue in fiction?" asked Sam. And right away I figured he'd had another late night with his sculpture and needed something to fill class time. Unless this was the kind of thing he thought about as he chiseled away at the block of wood in his studio.

"There isn't any," said Cissy, after a long silence that felt as if it was just going to keep on going.

"Oh?" said Sam, in that way that lets you know you're dead wrong. "How'd you get to school this morning, Cissy?"

"My mother drove me, because I overslept."

"And what'd you talk about?"

"Me oversleeping."

"What else?" said Sam.

"How my room needs cleaning, and Mom going to the store, and how she's out of dishwasher soap," said Cissy.

"And what would happen," said Sam, "if you put that into a story?"

Nobody said anything, but Winkle and Brenda and I all yawned at once. As if we'd been programmed.

"Exactly," said Sam. Then he was off on this long thing about dialogue in fiction being just like real-life conversation, with all the boring gunk taken out. And as he talked, I watched the way the sun made splotches on the floor in front of me. Sam raised his voice, the way he does when he's giving an assignment, and I heard him say, "Think of a conversation you've had recently, and for tomorrow write a dialogue the way it actually went, and that same conversation the way you'd write it in fiction."

And for once I didn't have any trouble knowing what to write.

Dialogue
The Way It Really Was

Martha: Hi, Sydney. I'm home.
Sydney: I don't care what she tells you—it isn't true.
Martha: Who?
Sydney: Mrs. Hubbard.
Martha: I haven't even <u>seen</u> Mrs. Hubbard.
Sydney: You will.
Martha: Can't you even say hello first? Can't I even take my coat off?
Sydney: Hello. But it's still not true.
Martha (sighing): What is it <u>this</u> time?
Sydney: It was this afternoon—when I got home from school—and . . .
Martha (sighing again): Just <u>tell</u> me what happened.
Sydney: I put a record on. I mean, Mom, it was so low I could hardly hear it and I was right in the same room, and all of a sudden Mrs. Hubbard starts banging on the floor with her broomstick—the one she rides on Halloween.

Martha: Sydney, stop that.

Sydney: See, there you go again. Taking her side against your very own daughter. When all I did was play a record. I don't see why we have to live here, anyway. I don't see why we can't have a place of our own.

Martha (sighing again): But we do live here, and if I've told you once I've told you a hundred times, it's not ideal, but it's okay for now.

Blah, blah, blah. Which just goes to show that S.K. knew what he was talking about when he said that every-day conversation was usually boring.

Dialogue
The Way I'd Write It in Fiction
(And the Way It Should Have Been)

Martha: Hi, Sydney, I'm home.

Sydney: Hey, Mom, don't believe anything Mrs. Hub-bard tells you. All I was doing was playing one of my Boomerang records, and right away she started banging on her ceiling, telling me to keep quiet.

Martha: Oh, honey, I'm so sorry. But I promise you it won't happen again. The reason I'm late is that I've been out looking at apartments. Real apartments, with our own front door, with a lock and key, and with no Mrs. Hubbard.

Sydney: And where I can have a dog?

Martha: Yes.

Sydney: And parties?
Martha: Yes.
Sydney: And play my records?
Martha: As loud as you want. After all, what's the use of having a Boomerang for a father if you can't listen to his music?

April

"April fool," said Porter after I'd reached up to see if there really *was* a caterpillar in my hair.

We were sitting on Mrs. Hubbard's back steps, and so far he'd tricked me three times already. Once, by tripping over a wheelbarrow and positively writhing on the ground until I was all set to call an *ambulance*. And then by telling me I had a hole in my jeans. And now with that dumb old caterpillar that wasn't.

"April smapril fool smool," said Porter, hopping up and down the steps on one foot.

"Yeah," I said.

He switched to the other leg and hopped along the

path by the side of the rose bed, looking back to say, "And guess what else?"

"I know. April fool." And when I didn't say anything else, he turned and disappeared through the hedge. Then, because the sun was warm and there was the buzzing of a chain saw somewhere in the neighborhood, and today'd been the last day of school before spring vacation, I leaned my elbows on the next step up, let my head fall back, and sort of drifted, watching the squiggles on the insides of my eyes.

Until I felt a presence and looked up to see this giant standing in front of me. (Actually, he was more like a string bean.)

A string bean who said, "Barracuda breath, I presume."

"Huh?" I said.

"You're outspoken, if nothing else," he said.

And right away I began fiddling with my hair and stuffing my shirttail into my pants, because when a person tells you you're something, "if nothing else," it definitely means there's a lot wrong with the rest of you.

Except that all of a sudden I wondered what this person was doing in my back yard, and why I was letting him insult me.

"The key to the garage is on a hook under the steps," I said, having ruled out meter reader (too young) and ax murderer (something about the freckles—and I know that's a really dumb remark; for all I know Lizzie Borden may have had freckles). Anyway, by then I'd decided he was somebody Mrs. Hubbard'd found to work in her garden. "You and the other worms should hit it off just fine," I said, getting up and starting for the back door.

"One *worm* body's as good as another," the string bean said.

I sat down on the step again, trying to think why that sounded like something I'd heard before. And just then Porter came barreling out of the hedge and jumped on the back of the boy, who hardly seemed to notice, except for bending his knees a little.

"Wally Martin," I said, looking hard at my tennis shoes, remembering the letter I'd written, and trying to think of a way to self-destruct. But when I couldn't manage that, I said as snidely as I could (because I've always wanted to say something really snide), "It's *warm* body. One *warm* body's as good as another. Except that it's not and *that's* the point."

"It was a pun," said Wally String Bean.

Which, of course, would've led me to say how Sam Klemkoski'd said that puns were the lowest form of humor, except that just then Mrs. Hubbard started rapping on the window.

"Your grandmother wants you," said Wally Martin.

"She's *not* my grandmother."

"Yeah," said Porter. "Sydney's got Boomerang blood."

"I'll bet," said Wally.

"Smoomerang blood," said Porter.

"Tell me about it," said Wally in a way that meant, "Tell me, but don't expect me to believe you."

"So what about this Boomerang blood of yours?" said Wally Martin the next day, when he *was* actually working in Mrs. Hubbard's garden. That's on account of the day before: when Mrs. H. was banging on the window, it wasn't (for once) to say there was too much noise but because she was trying to nab Wally. I mean, she came running out the back door and asked him if he would do an old lady a favor and help with a little yard work, saying she'd pay him three dollars an hour and that he could work with *me*, who, because I lived there, would certainly want to help. Anyway, if there was one thing she believed, it was that families should help each other out.

"I'm *not* her family," I said later that night, when Mom and I were having supper at Sam's studio. "And why should *I* work for nothing when Wally Martin's getting *paid*?" I said, as I bit down on my egg roll.

"Because it's the decent thing to do," said my mother, the master of nice.

"Horsefeathers," said Sam.

"And we *do* live there," said Lady McWimp.

"That's just the problem," I said.

"Sydney's right," said Sam, stabbing a Styrofoam box with a plastic knife. "Why *should* she? Any more than either one of you should be spied on, told not to run a bath after nine at night, shushed if you so much as breathe, and evacuated from your digs so your landlady can have a party."

"She doesn't think of herself as a landlady," said my mother.

"She *is* a landlady," said Sam.

"Don't you believe in people helping people?"

"This's got nothing to do with help."

All of a sudden my egg roll tasted cold and soggy and as if it might stick in my throat. I got up, moving over to Sam's sculpture, which was turning into something pretty awesome and which I will definitely get back to.

So there I was the next day, yanking at stalks of bamboo in Mrs. Hubbard's yard and pretending with every yank that it was hair from her head.

"About the Boomerang blood," said Wally Martin again. "Tell me about it."

"There's nothing to tell," I said. "It just is."

"Is what?"

"There."

"Where?"

"In my veins," I said.

"*Sure* it is," he said.

"It is, *too*," said Porter, who had come to stand between the two of us, "if Sydney says."

"Now I get it," said Wally. "Sydney Downie: *Sydney Downie Down Down.*"

"Uh-huh."

"And next you're going to tell me you're some Boomerang's kid."

"Uh-huh."

"Kid smid," said Porter.

"Whose?" said Wally.

"Jamie's," I said.

"Oh, right," said Wally. "And that explains what you're doing pulling up crud out of a back yard *here*, rather than living big, on a cattle station in Australia with Jamie."

"The outback's so isolated, and so far. Anyway, we like it *here*. I mean, it's not ideal, but it's okay for now." I stood there hearing my mother's words coming out of my mouth and feeling clammy and shaky all over. I clapped my hand over my mouth and rubbed my lips, as if I could wipe away what I'd said. Then I tugged at a bamboo stalk that refused to budge.

"What's an outback?" said Porter. "Outback, smout—"

"Don't say it," said Wally. "Don't even *think* it."

"Outback smoutback," whispered Porter under his breath.

"And since Molly's still in residence *there*, at least as far as I know, then *your* mother must've been an earlier wife. Way earlier, and one nobody ever heard of. Is that right?" said Wally. And for a minute I struggled against hearing the name of the wife I'd somehow always managed to slide over when I was reading about Jamie.

"My mother's a very private person," I said. "Her name

is Martha and she never wanted anything to do with the limelight."

"Give me a break," said Wally.

"Break smeak," said Porter.

"Can't you go somewhere?" said Wally, looking down at his brother. "Can't you find someone to *play* with?"

"How about you? It's the least you can do," I said, turning on my heel through a winter's worth of decayed leaves (in a way that even Nat the Gat would've been proud of) and dragging my rake around to the front of the house.

It struck me that what I had here were more scraps of dialogue. The kind Sam said to listen for at the beginning of the year. And if these particular scraps sounded contentious (a word I've been waiting to use), it was because Wally Martin and I hadn't gotten off to a terrific start, although if *he* hadn't been such a rotten brother to Porter and if *I* hadn't told him so in my letter, *and* if I just saw him in line at the pizzeria or at the beach, I'd definitely look *twice*.

The thing about a journal is that sometimes you can say things that don't exactly fit in—which is why I now have to write about Sam's sculpture. Between the last time I'd seen it and egg-roll night, all the ripply gouge marks in the wood had been smoothed out, and there was something about it that made me want to put my arms around the figure and just stand there holding on to it. The way I feel sometimes about a tree. Which I guess is what Sam's sculpture actually is. A tree.

The day after the second scrap of dialogue, it rained and I went to the mall with Cissy. She called early that morning to see what I was doing and actually managed to make it through the whole day without once saying, "Natalie says . . ." Which then made me feel honor-bound, when we saw this grossly disgusting outfit with little puffy pink sleeves in the window of The Fashion Bug, *not* to say that it looked like something Nat the Gat would wear.

It rained the day after that, too, and the day after and the day after *that*. Once, when Sam K. called my mother, I answered the phone and was complaining about it and he said, "Well, you know what Eliot said." I said, "Eliot who?" and Sam sighed and said, "Look it up in Bartlett's *Familiar Quotations*, Sydney." Which I did (what *else* was there to do?) and found it was T. S. Eliot, and what he said was "April is the cruelest month." Which I thought was absolutely right.

Not just on account of it being spring vacation with me stuck in the house, Cissy off visiting her aunt, Mary Jo in New Jersey, and Porter home with Wally and not even needing a baby-sitter *because* of Wally, and Wally there because of *me* writing him that letter.

But because of what happened between Mom and Sam Klemkoski.

Which was directly related to the weather (unless, like me, you happen to think Nat the Gat's really a witch, and after predicting that some night my mother wouldn't come home, she then *made* it happen).

Anyway, one night my mother (my mother!) didn't come home.

It was at the height of the storm, which the TV weathermen were now calling a northeaster. That particular afternoon Mom's car was in the shop, so she had taken the bus downtown to do some work in the main library and was going up to Sam's afterward for supper. Then he was going to bring her home.

Except that he didn't.

Except that late at night (it was almost at the end of *Midnight Mystery*) Mom called and said that Sam's car wouldn't start and she'd never get a cab in all this rain so she guessed she'd better sleep over at Sam's.

Sleep over?

Then she told me not to worry because Mrs. Hubbard was right downstairs, and I said why should I worry, all the while looking over my shoulder and wishing the wind would stop howling and wondering what I'd do if the lights went out.

"You don't have your nightgown," I blurted out. "Or even a toothbrush."

"Good grief, Sydney, I'll sleep in my clothes. Stop acting like my mother," my mother said.

Right away my face burned, and I felt incredibly dumb and couldn't wait to hang up so she wouldn't hear how I looked.

And it occurred to me that these times my mother spent with Sam were actually dates and that it's very difficult being the daughter of a dating mother.

Anyway, I woke the next morning to bright sunshine and the sort of washed look everything gets after a storm. And to the sound of Mrs. Hubbard's voice saying, "What do you mean coming in here at this hour of the morning, when I know full well you've been out all night?"

I thought she was talking to Dimples, except that it was my mother who answered. "With all that rain, Sam's car wouldn't start. I called Sydney to tell her, though I didn't think to ask her to let you know. I hope you didn't worry." The whole time she was talking, my mother was smoothing things: her hair, her sweater, her skirt. And in back of her, Sam was bristling. (And, of course, *I* was hanging over the banister, where I'd been since I realized Mrs. H. wasn't talking to the cat.)

"Worry has nothing to do with it," Mrs. Hubbard sniffed.

"Well, then . . ."

"It's just that in *our* family we don't *do* things like that," Mrs. Hubbard went on.

"Like what?" boomed Sam.

"But we're *not* your family, we just live here," my mother said.

"Well, of course you are, my dear," said Mrs. Hubbard. "You *know* we don't have tenants in this neighborhood."

"Horsefeathers," said Sam.

"Well, really," said Mrs. H.

"Sam, just let me handle this, please," my mother said.

"So handle."

"I will—later."

"And to think you have a daughter of an impressionable age," said Mrs. Hubbard.

Who, me?

"Who, Sydney?" said Sam, nudging Mom to get her started up the steps again. At which point I flew off the railing, and was sitting on the couch when the two of them came into the living room.

"Hi, guys," I said, aiming for a combination of casual and worldly-wise (as if it was no big deal that my mother had just spent the night with Sam Klemkoski).

"Sam, I *said* I'd handle it," hissed my mother. "You didn't have to be rude."

"Rude? Rude? You come in here and right away that old biddy accuses you of shacking up, and you tell me I'm *rude*?"

"She didn't accuse me of shacking up. She just said—"

"Ask Sydney."

"Leave Sydney out of this."

"Hi, guys," I said again.

Creak went the next-to-the-bottom step.

"Shhhh," said my mother. "She's listening."

"Who? Your non-rude non-landlady, who's even now creeping up the stairs?"

"Why are you *doing* this?"

"Doing what?"

"Why are you making trouble like this?" My mother's face looked as if maybe it was going to crumble.

"Trouble? I'm making trouble?" said Sam.

"You're deliberately starting a fight."

"A fight? There's not enough privacy in this place to *have* a fight."

I was moving my head back and forth like someone watching a tennis match.

"Keep your voice down. She'll hear you," my mother said.

"She" Mrs. Hubbard or "she" me? I wondered as their words flew around me.

"What the bloody hell's my voice got to do with it?" bellowed Sam Klemkoski. "It's your peace-at-any-cost life that's the problem."

"Well, it's *my* life and—"

"And you've done a royal job of screwing it up. Your kid thinks she's a Boomerang—"

"You encouraged her."

"*You* never told her anything about her *real* father. What do you expect. Any fool knows a kid needs—"

"So now you're an expert on *children*. I thought it was only blocks of wood you . . ."

I pulled my knees up under my chin, trying to make myself smaller, though it was pretty obvious Mom and Sam didn't seem to notice I was there. Part of me wanted to slither down under the sofa cushions, because fights sometimes give me a stomachache. And part of me was busy pretending I was a regular person with a regular mother and father having a regular fight. And just as I was trying to decide whether they would kiss and make up (like Cissy's parents always did), or get a divorce (like Winkle Shultz's), I was yanked back into the present.

"You ought to know by now what's important to your own daughter," Sam was saying. "She's laid it out for the entire creative-writing class to see: she wants a real place to live, with a real front door, a lock and a key, and *no* Mrs. Hubbard."

"It's not up to *you*," said my mother, her voice spiraling for once, and breaking loose.

Suddenly I was mad clear through. At Mom for not understanding, and at Sam for betraying me. I jumped up and ran out of the room and into my bedroom, slamming the door behind me. I turned the stereo up as high as it would go, put on the first side of *Sydney Downie Down Down*, and dropped the needle onto the second band. I listened to "In the Land of Never Never," the song I was sure my father had written for my mother—that Jamie had written for Martha.

Thump thump thump, Mrs. Hubbard was banging on her ceiling.

"See what I mean," yelled Sam. I heard him run down the stairs and out the front door.

And from the living room, a hicuppy sniffling sound. I crept back in to see my mother sitting on the couch, crying. When she saw me, she blinked for a minute and said, "Now see what you've done."

Thump thump thump went Mrs. Hubbard down below.

And right then I decided T. S. Eliot knew what he was talking about. April was lousy.

And it didn't get any better when I went back to school after spring break and Nat the Gat greeted me with "Well, Boomerang bunny, how was your Easter?"

"Okay," I said, thinking how the best part of the vacation had been not having to see *her.*

We were all sitting around the lunchroom, and she leaned across a tray of soggy french fries to say, "Any news?"

"News?" I said.

"Family news."

"Family news?"

"Stop repeating everything I say, and tell us what happened," said Nat. "And don't say 'What happened?' "

"What happened?" said Cissy.

"About Sam Klemkoski and how he looks positively ravaged. As if maybe he has a broken heart."

"What happened?" said Mary Jo and Winkle Shultz at the same time.

"When I saw your mother in history this morning, she wasn't herself. All pale, with watery eyes," said Nat the Gat.

"What happened?" said Janet Preller.

Then suddenly it was as though I was on the top of an icy hill, trying to keep from going over but sliding, sliding. "They had a fight," I heard myself saying.

"A fight?" And everybody leaned closer over the soggy french fries. "Was it a big fight?"

"I'm not sure," I said, because having lived with my mother all these years, there'd never been much to compare it with. "Big enough, I guess."

"Does he call?" asked Natalie Gatling.

"No," I said, remembering the silence in the house the last few days.

"Does *she* call *him*?" asked Cissy.

"I don't *think* so," I said. "But last night she sent me to the basement to do a half a load of wash and told me to look for my missing green socks while I was there, and when I came back upstairs, she sort of jumped away from the phone. But I don't think she actually called."

"Probably not," agreed Mary Jo.

"What'd they fight *about?*"

"Well, it rained and the car wouldn't start and my mother couldn't get home and then the next morning—"

"I told you she'd start staying out all night," said Nat the Gat.

"Let Sydney tell it," said Cissy.

"—when they *did* get home, Mrs. Hubbard freaked out."

"I'll bet he wants her to move in with him," said Winkle.

"No," I said. "He wants us to move out of where we are now," I said.

"Yeah, and him with that great big house. You could live there, Sydney. In Sam Klemkoski's house."

"You have to admit you've thought about it," said Cissy.

And for just about the first time, I admitted to myself that I *had* thought about it. Not so much my *mother* moving into Sam's house, but *me* moving in. Me settled up on the third floor, with plenty of space downstairs for parties, and a dog.

"Well, it's up to you to *do* something," said Nat the Gat, breaking in on my thoughts. "I mean, you owe it to the rest of us. Otherwise, we're going to be stuck with *two* lovesick, distracted, grouchy teachers."

"Yeah," said the rest of the Grecian chorus around the lunch table.

"You could make him jealous. Make him think some

tall, handsome, and exotic man is madly in love with
your mother."

"One was," I said, sort of under my breath.

"What?" said Nat the Gat.

"Nothing," I said.

But when we got to creative writing that afternoon Sam
was ravaged-looking, and I knew right off that I had to
do something to get him and my mother back together.
I just didn't know what.

Conclusion
Jamie and Martha: Destiny

"None of it's important," said Jamie Ward to Martha
Foley one afternoon when they were walking in the Royal
Botanic Gardens in Sydney. "I don't care about the
crowds or the noise or the fame. I don't even care about
being a Boomerang. All I care about is <u>you</u>."

"Oh, Jamie," said Martha. "Do you mean it?"

"Yes," said Jamie. "I want to marry you and keep you
safe, away from the crowds and the noise and the fame."

"Oh, Jamie," said Martha, "this is the happiest day of
my life. And <u>no one</u> will ever mean as much to me as
you do."

Note from Sam Klemkoski to Sydney Downie: *As a
short story, this lacks plot development. And credibility.*

* * *

It was bad enough having to deal with my mother's broken heart at home, but then to have to put up with Sam Klemkoski at school was even worse. I mean, Nat the Gat was right: Sam was distracted, and grouchy. I wasn't sure about lovesick, though, because you never know about artists. I mean, I didn't know whether he was acting this way on account of my mother or because his work wasn't going well. Or if his work wasn't going well because of my mother.

Meanwhile, he glowered and grumped and never, even though it was spring and he was wearing sandals again, twiddled his toes. One day, we went into class and Sam had written AND THEN SHE SAID . . . across the top of the blackboard.

"Said what?" said Cissy.

"You tell me," said Sam, and even though he was looking at the transom over the door when he said it, I had the feeling he was speaking to me. Like maybe this whole assignment was so Sam could find out what my mother said about him (nothing—she was into the "stiff upper lip" routine). Which in turn reminded me of the way Janet Preller was always asking different people what this guy she liked at Milton High said about *her*.

Suddenly I felt used and decided Mom and Sam K. were going to have to work these things out on their own. I changed the title slightly and started to write.

And Then <u>He</u> Said

And then he said, "What'd you write me that letter for?" and it was as if I'd been waiting all during Wally Martin's spring break for the other shoe to drop. And it finally had.

It was the last day before Wally went back to school and we were working again in Mrs. Hubbard's yard, which was full of mud that Porter kept jumping in and splattering everything in sight with (mostly me).

"Because," I said, sort of scraping the thoughts together in my head and trying to think of a polite way to tell him he was a rotten brother, that everybody in his family was too much into doing his own thing, and that I felt sorry for Porter.

"Because you're a rotten brother and your family's too interested in doing stuff and going places, and nobody pays any attention to Porter, who's an okay kid. Except that if he splashes mud on me one more time, I'll kill him."

"Barracuda breath," said Wally, in a way that made it hard for me to tell whether he meant it or not. "It's none of your business."

"Except it *is*. Because Porter's my friend."

"Friend smiend," said Porter, coming up in back of me.

"And what you don't understand," said Wally, "is that when Mom and Dad were little, neither one of them had

<u>anything</u>. *I mean, we're talking major poor, and now that my dad's made some money, you're right, they want to do stuff and go places."*

"Except—"

"Yeah, I know all the excepts, and I told them and they both nodded and said 'Uh-huh' and that all they wanted was for me and Porter to be happy and how they'd try to change. But grown-ups usually don't change."

And I nodded <u>my</u> head, wondering if I'd've had the nerve to tell his parents what Wally told them, and thinking how my mother wasn't so quick to change either, and that I was never going to get that way.

Then all of a sudden Wally and I were talking about other stuff: music and the Boomerangs and the books of his I still had; about movies we'd seen, and how neither one of us could stand the Three Stooges; and how before long it would be summer. When we finished in the yard and he'd gotten paid, we took Porter and walked over to the mall and had pizza and Cokes (because Wally said it wasn't fair that he got paid and I didn't). After that, we went into a record store and got the new Jamie Ward album, "Jamie Alone," because Wally said I should hear it and that we'd share it and start off keeping it at my house on account of his being away at school.

When we got back home and it was time to go in, we stood around for a while, neither one of us moving. Wally said it hadn't been too bad being home over spring break instead of someplace else, and how maybe he wouldn't go to camp this summer, but get a job here in town. His mouth twitched when he said it and I got the feeling he was giving it serious thought.

Finally I went inside and played the record, liking the way it sounded—haunting and gentle and sort of electrically charged. Then, because Mrs. Hubbard wasn't home, I turned the volume up and listened to it all the way through again.

May

It wasn't that Nat the Gat and I were getting along any better, or that I still didn't want to gag each time I thought how she had a different Swatch for every day of the week. It's just that Hawthorne Hills is a small school, and in a small school there aren't *that* many crowds. In our class there were basically only two: ours (or lately, N. the G.'s) and Chritbelle Critten's, where everybody seemed to wear dirty underwear (I know from gym class) and smell sort of stale. Either that or be a loner, which gets lonely at times. Which explains why we were all (Cissy, Mary Jo, Winkle, Janet, Brenda, and Natalie Gatling and I) sitting in a row on the hill in back of the main building after school one day early in May.

We were sitting on the hill pretending not to sunbathe (because of the ozone) and feeling glum because we had just come from Sam's class, which was even glummer than Sam's classes have recently been. And boring, too. I mean, when Mary Jo read her homework out loud (lately he's been into having us read stuff out loud, which definitely cuts down on what he, as teacher, has to do), Sam said she had used a pathetic fallacy. And when somebody said, "What's that?" he said, "Look it up." He didn't even give us one of his mile-long explanations so that you knew, by the time he was finished, that you'd *never* forget whatever it was you were never to forget.

(Pathetic fallacy: something to do with writers of impassioned prose who give things in nature the emotions of humans. At least according to Thrall and Hibbard.)

"If you're not going to do something, Sydney, I'll have to take care of it myself," said Nat the Gat from the other end of the row. (Even if Natalie Gatling and I have to coexist, we don't have to sit *next* to each other.)

"Do something about what?" I said.

"Your mother."

"My mother?"

"Your mother and Sam Klemkoski."

"My mother and Sam Klemkoski?"

"You're doing it again," said N. the G. "Stop repeating and get on with it."

And before I could ask what I could possibly do about

my mother and Sam Klemkoski (without admitting I'd tried and failed), everybody started to talk.

"Today's class was a bummer," said Janet.

"The pits," said Mary Jo.

"A regular yawn," said Winkle.

"And to think this was going to be my favorite class," said Cissy.

"And it would've been, too, if Carol Weatherby was still here from last year," said Brenda.

And it suddenly occurred to me that, on account of liking Sam, it'd been a long time since I'd actually thought of Carol Weatherby.

"It's obvious I'm just going to have to take things into my own hands," said Nat the Gat, holding her hands out and turning them this way and that—I guess to show us how capable they were. (Though how could hands with mile-long stick-on silver nails be capable of anything?)

Then there was this sort of reverent (disgusting) silence while everybody (except me) in the row leaned forward and looked at Gnat.

"Yes," she said, as if following stage directions that called for a significant pause. "It's obvious," she said again, this time with emphasis. "My Aunt Clara's coming to town for a visit and I think I'll ask my mother if we can have Sam Klemkoski for dinner so the two of them can meet. My Aunt Clara's gorgeous—with long blond hair and a year-round tan—and she has a real thing for underdogs. I mean, she'd positively take him in hand:

she'd make him get real shoes and real clothes, and stop going around looking like a ragman, and live in a *real* house instead of that thing Sydney described."

Now, right away I knew *I'd* never told Natalie Gatling anything about Sam's house. And judging by the way my bigmouthed sometime friend Cissy turned beet red, she knew it, too. "I think Sam's kind of cute," she said, I guess to make it up to me.

"Well, my mother won't," said N. the G. "My mother'll positively *die* when she sees him, but I'll just have to explain it's for the good of the cause and that we can't bear to sit through any more of those dreadful classes. And besides, once Aunt Clara gets her hands on him, he'll be almost presentable."

Presentable? Sam?

Real clothes? Real shoes?

And a real house?

And all of a sudden I got this humongous pain in my stomach. I mean, it hurt just thinking about Sam in Natalie Gatling's Aunt Clara's clutches, when I was sure what he really wanted was *my mother*. The same as I was sure that what *she* really wanted was Sam Klemkoski.

And it was up to me to do something about it.

But what?

I went home by way of the mall so I could get a giant chocolate-chip cookie and a Diet Coke and have time to think about what to do. I thought of the books I'd read, and the movies, and the TV shows. All the love stories where the hero and heroine met and fell in love and fought and split up and then got back together again.

Except that my mind kept tripping over the idea of Sam and my mother as hero and heroine.

Besides that, in almost everything I could think of, the main couple were young. Or at least not somebody's mother, somebody's teacher.

Then I figured what I'd have to do was adapt.

I got another cookie (I adapt better when I'm eating) and played the old game I used to play whenever I lost something important: If I were my keys/glasses/pen, where would I be? Only this time I thought, If I were suffering from a broken heart, how would I want someone to help me? Which was hard to answer because I'd never exactly suffered from a broken heart (Jeff Clark in eighth grade doesn't really count). Then I asked myself if Wally Martin (who had already written me two letters from school) didn't write again, *then* would I be brokenhearted, and what would I want someone to do for me? Except that made me start thinking about things I'd forgotten to put in the letter I'd just sent him and not about Mom and Sam at all.

So I had to resort to hearsay. I mean, between Janet Preller and some of the juniors and seniors I'd listened to in the lunchroom, I ought to have known all the tricks: anonymous letters, anonymous phone calls, anonymous flowers; planning a party to get them together; arranging it so they ran into each other in a totally deserted place where there was no way out for at least six hours.

Except that none of these seemed appropriate for my mother and Sam Klemkoski.

I kept on thinking all the way home (when I wasn't thinking about my stomach; I had definitely OD'd on cookies), and when I got there I just walked up the stairs and into our living room, where Mom was correcting papers, and said, "Hey, Mom. Why don't we move?"

And the weird thing was that she looked at me as if I'd said something utterly brilliant and said, "Oh, do you think so, Sydney?"

"Yeah, Mom, I think so," I said. "I mean, you've been sort of down lately and . . . ."

I needn't've wasted my breath, because Mom kept nodding her head and saying, "Yes, yes, we could. We don't *have* to live here. Sydney, you're a genius." Then she went right out (with her slippers on), got a newspaper, came back, started reading ads out loud, circling things, and making lists. And looking up from time to time as if I *were* some kind of genius for having suggested it. All I could think of was that everything I'd been saying for about a thousand years had finally made an impression. Or maybe it was the things Sam had said.

Now I admit that none of this was getting my mother and Sam K. back together but, the way I looked at it, if she was going to be brokenhearted, she could just as well be brokenhearted in a place of our own.

Besides that, I was still working on it, and tomorrow I planned to tackle Sam.

I found him in his classroom the next day, when everyone (students *and* teachers) was supposed to be at assembly in the Big Hall, and I didn't know what I was going to say until I opened my mouth.

"Honesty is the best policy, as Mrs. Hubbard, who is probably the cause of this whole problem, sometimes says," I said.

"Except when it doesn't suit her," said Sam.

"And I know it's none of my business, except that it is in a way, so I have to tell you my mother's looking for an apartment, where she can have privacy and guests and even fights. And without actually putting words in her mouth, I *know* she'd like to see you and maybe you could offer to help her move—"

"Love me, love my van," said Sam.

"And that way you could both . . . I mean, the two of you could . . . well, you know. And besides, if you don't, Natalie Gatling's going to have her mother invite you to dinner so you can meet her Aunt Clara, who specializes in underdogs and who'll make you dress like everybody else and wear real shoes."

"Not the dreaded Aunt Clara," said Sam.

"You know Aunt Clara?"

"The world is full of them and I've met my share,"

said Sam. After that, he looked worried and didn't say anything, and I thought maybe he wasn't going to, ever again.

"About the fight," I said, beginning to think that skipping assembly (and maybe getting caught) wouldn't be worth it after all, "you could pretend it never happened."

"Simplistic," said Sam.

"And go on from there."

"Moving, did you say?" said Sam, after a while. "Well, maybe I'd better . . ."

"Without actually telling her I told you," I said.

"Without actually telling her," said Sam, heading for the teachers' room, where I happened to know my mother was sitting out the assembly. But how did he?

Now, the thing is, if this were a romance novel (even one about a mother and a teacher), the two of them would ride off into the sunset, pausing just long enough to tell me they were getting married and that we'd all live happily ever after in the converted bakery. Except that it didn't work that way, because in all the years I've known her, Mom's never rushed into anything. But they did go back to eating Chinese and laughing in the halls. Their classes (his English and her history) got better. And from the very beginning, Mom would only look at apartments that advertised "No lease required."

*   *   *

But as for me, I ended up feeling sort of cheated—as if I'd been reading a book, and when I got to the climax, the pages were missing.

I have come to a conclusion: Even if I have to use up an entire Magic Marker censoring my journal, I'm not handing it in the way it is now. I mean, who'd ever've thought, way back in September when we started, that *my* self-awareness would be so involved with *Sam's.*

"I don't know what you did, Sydney," said Nat the Gat, "but when my mother called Sam Klemkoski to invite him for dinner, he said he was booked solid from now till the end of the year. Which wasn't exactly fair to Aunt Clara, who couldn't wait to meet him and would've done wonders for him."

"Get off Sydney's back," said Cissy. "Whatever she did worked, didn't it?"

"Yeah," said Mary Jo. "Creative writing's halfway decent again, and Sam was picking violets over by the hill at lunchtime."

"Well, pardon me, I'm sure," said Gnat. "I forgot this was 'Ask Sydney' time. Tell us what you did, Boomerang buddy."

And much as I wanted to, I didn't. Mostly, I think, because some things are nobody's business.

*   *   *

When I got home that afternoon, Mom had come in and gone out again, but the violets were on the windowsill in a clear glass bowl. I stood in front of them for a minute, just touching them with my fingertip and feeling that lumpy, sad way I sometimes feel in the spring, which may be what people mean by spring fever. Then I went into my room to do my creative-writing homework, which, as Sam's assignments had been going lately, was a pretty good one.

A Step out of Time

I stepped into my time machine and suddenly it was . . .

Actually, Sam had given us the beginning of the first sentence and told us to use it as a means of exploring a time that really interested us. He said to be sure, when we came back to the present at the end of the paper, to compare and contrast the two times.

A Step out of Time

I stepped into my time machine and suddenly it was the sixties and there was a lot going on and I was right there in the middle of it all. The weird part was that when I opened the door of my time machine and stepped outside, it was as if everything that had taken place during that decade was happening again for my benefit. The good and the bad. The happy and the sad.

There was John F. Kennedy being sworn in as President and saying, "Ask not what your country can do for you; ask what you can do for your country," and at the same time there was John F. Kennedy being assassinated. There was his wife who was so incredibly brave, those little children, and that riderless horse.

There were people who were committed to things: peace, love, black power. There was also flower power.

And, in the late sixties, there were the Boomerangs.

During the sixties, people lived in communes. They had sit-ins and love-ins and went to jail, and some of them went to fight a war in Vietnam. And some of them didn't. They called themselves hippies and played guitars and made music and went to Woodstock. Others went to the East Village in New York, and to Haight-Ashbury in California.

And then there were the Boomerangs—four great-looking rock singers from Australia named Clive, Oscar, Jamie, and Pudge. Soon, everyone was singing songs like "In the Land of Never Never" and "Every Morning" and shouting "A-va-go."

In the sixties, there were beads and miniskirts and boots. There were jeans and long skirts. There were drugs and psychedelic experiences and people saying "Wow!" and "Peace."

And there were the Boomerangs.

In the sixties, people cared intensely about things. Even about things they didn't want to do. Which is a way I think people ought to feel.

After a while, I went back to my time machine and climbed inside, except that something was wrong. I couldn't get back.

I can't get back.

When I finished what I was writing, there were tears running down my face and I wiped them with my sleeve.

The day Sam gave the "Step out of Time" papers back, he didn't give me mine. Instead, he told me to stay after class, and when everyone had gone, he just stood there for the longest time, looking out the window and twisting my rolled-up paper. Suddenly he turned around, slapping my paper down on the side of a desk and saying, "Enough already, Sydney. Enough already." His voice was sort of harsh and angry, the way I know Sam tends to sound when he really cares about something. And I liked how his sounding that way made me feel.

Then, instead of giving me my paper, he folded it, stuffed it in his back pocket, and told me, with his voice still rough and scratchy, to hurry up so I wouldn't be late for my next class.

Watching my mother look for an apartment was like watching her inch her way into the twentieth century.

Not that I actually went with her *to* look, but I saw her when she came home *from* looking. And it's not that I didn't want to go, or that she ever told me not to, but it was always a kind of unwritten rule: My mother had to find an apartment on her own.

And some days I thought she never would. Some days she'd come in looking almost gray and talk about small closets and tiny kitchens and old-fashioned plumbing. About halls that smelled of cabbage and had no cross ventilation. (As if where we were living now was the Taj Mahal.) There were times when I caught her gazing longingly at our living room that used to be a porch and which had never, in my entire life, been painted and was still a revolting green. I even heard her tell Dimples she'd miss him (her?).

And Mrs. Hubbard wasn't making life any easier. She sniffed and sighed a lot, and talked about ingratitude, muttering something about a serpent's tooth and a thankless child. Then one day she brought a mousy-looking woman with seams in her stockings upstairs to look at the apartment, and later that day Mrs. H. told Mom that her "cousin" would move in just as soon as we found a place of our own.

Which we did. A two-bedroom apartment that was farther downtown than we are now but not as far down as Sam. Mom went to see it and came right home and got me and took me back to look at it. And I knew, because of the door downstairs that you had to open with a key, and because of the door *upstairs* that you had to open with a key, that this was the place for us. The apartment itself had two bedrooms—one large and one small (mine)—but with its own porch, a living room, a dining room, and a kitchen so narrow that if Mom and I were both in it at the same time we had to walk sideways, but where all the shelves, drawers, and cupboards were *ours*.

And it was empty and ready for us to move in.

For a while we explored it, peering into closets, flushing the toilet, and opening and closing the door to the medicine chest. We called to each other from the far reaches of the apartment and listened to the way our voices sort of echoed. Back in the living room again, we danced up and down the bare wood floors and looked out the windows at the football field of the college across the street.

"Oh," said my mother, sitting down on the floor and holding her jaw as if she had a toothache. "We don't *own* anything," she said.

"Oh," I said, sitting down next to her and thinking how everything we'd sat on and slept on and used for all those years had belonged to Mrs. Hubbard.

"Except the director's chair in your bedroom," I reminded my mother. "And the wicker magazine rack in the living room."

"And the bookcases."

"And the books."

"Well," said Mom, "we'll just have to get some things."

Which we did. The next Saturday. Because, as it turned out, Sam was an authority on garage sales, and he followed us around in his van as we gathered up used everything: rugs and dishes, a table and four straight chairs, a couch that looked almost new, and two chests of drawers. Everything except beds, because my mother said she'd sit up all night before she'd sleep on a secondhand bed. We went to the Mattress Barn.

We packed all the stuff in our old place that belonged to us: our clothes and books and snow boots, my dolls from when I was little, which I'd put in the back of a closet. Then Mom remembered a couple of boxes she'd stored in Mrs. Hubbard's basement for years and which I'd never known about. She brought them up one day and poked around inside them enough to see that they were her notes and books from her year of graduate school in Australia; then she shoved them in a corner, said she'd get to them one day, and went back to school for a faculty meeting.

For a while after my mother left, I just sat around the apartment listening to the Jamie Ward album Wally and I were sharing and feeling a lot of mixed-up feelings. Like how I was glad we were moving and that after next week I'd never wake up again to the sound of Mrs. Hubbard thumping around downstairs after those stupid birds and that I'd never again reach for something in the refrigerator and have to not eat it because it belonged to someone else. But in a way I was sad, too. I mean, I wouldn't be seeing as much of Porter Martin, even though his mother said I was their best baby-sitter ever and gave me a silver bracelet and said of course they'd still be using me. *And,* if Wally Martin really did stay home this summer (which he said he was going to do), then instead of being just on the other side of the hedge, I'd be a good ten minutes' walk away.

But then, as Mrs. Hubbard used to say sometimes (before she decided we had betrayed her and took to sighing a lot), "Absence makes the heart grow fonder."

Anyway, I turned the record over and was thinking all these things when, without meaning to, I started going through Mom's boxes. I sorted through textbooks that smelled musty and old notebooks where the pages were crowded with my mother's handwriting, except that it looked smaller and tighter than it does now and the ink had turned a funny shade of brown. I read some of her notes, but they were boring, and I flipped the pages to see if they got any better later on. Which is when I found the picture.

It was big, an eight-by-ten, and was of a young man

(his head and shoulders mostly). It was in black and white and sort of cracked around the edges. And it looked awesomely familiar.

I held it away at arm's length, and pulled it close. I tilted it this way and that, watching the lock of hair over one eye and how the light caught on his chin. Then all of a sudden, without knowing I was going to do it, I ran into the bathroom and stood in front of the mirror, holding the picture alongside my face, tracing the same cheekbones, the same nose, the same wide flat mouth, first on one and then on the other.

I was still standing there when my mother came in, and for a while she stood in the bathroom doorway, staring at me and the picture both in the mirror.

"You look like him," she said.

"He's—"

"Your father." She reached for the picture and carried it back into the living room, sitting on the edge of the couch and studying it as if she had just run into someone she hadn't seen for a long time. "Years ago I searched *everywhere* for this picture," Mom said. She stopped for a minute and made a face before going on. "Every place but the *right* place, I guess. But there was so much else to think about at the time."

After a while she got up and wandered around the room, holding the picture as if she didn't know what to do with it. I watched her, and when I couldn't stand watching her anymore, I reached for it and took it out of her hand and carried it into my room, tacking it up on the wall next to the Boomerangs, even though I knew it would have to come down in a day or so when I finished packing.

Later that night, after I'd heard Mrs. Hubbard shaking the cat-food box to try to get Dimples to come inside, and after Mom'd knocked on my door to ask if I was all right and I'd said I was, and when the neighborhood was into that middle-of-the-night kind of quiet, I got out my notebook and decided to finish my short story.

Conclusion
Jamie and Martha: Destiny

The crowds were swarming and shoving all around them, and Jamie was busy shaking hands and signing autographs.

"It means a lot to you, doesn't it?" said Martha Foley as she tried to keep from being swallowed up in the crowd. "It's important to you, isn't it?"

"The Boomerangs are important," said Jamie. "They mean a great deal to people. But I want for you to be a part of it all with me. You want that, too, don't you, Martha?"

For a minute the young American girl with the long brown hair didn't say anything. Then, slowly, she shook her head as she said, "Jamie, I think there's something you should know."

"What is it?" said Jamie, pushing at the crowd to try

and clear a space around him and Martha. *"Don't tell me there's—"*

"There's someone else," said Martha. *"I'm sorry to have to tell you like this but—"*

"Who is he?" said Jamie.

"His name is Arthur Downie and he's a student at the university, and I hope that someday he'll be my husband. And the father of my children."

"Well, Martha," said Jamie, turning away to sign another autograph, *"I only want for you to be happy. But remember, I'll never forget you."*

"I'll never forget you either," said Martha, calling over her shoulder as she pushed her way through the crowd on her way back to Arthur Downie.

June

We moved in over the Memorial Day weekend and now it's June and we're settled into our apartment and there're a whole new set of noises we're getting used to: the way the bus sounds as it pulls away from the curb, the *scritch-scratch* of the poodle's toenails on the bare floor in the apartment upstairs, and the way our toilet sort of gulps when anyone else in the building flushes theirs.

We're learning the tricks of the stove and the best time of day to use the laundry machines in the basement and that the mailman sometimes gets the mail in the wrong boxes but that it all evens out in the end. At night, before I go to bed, I stand out on my porch and look at all the windows across the way and wonder about the people in those other apartments, and then sometimes I pretend I'm the last person left on earth except for Wally Martin, but he's at his school in New Hampshire and somehow we have to work our way toward each other.

As for my mother—she's adjusting well, though truth to tell (as Mrs. Hubbard used to say), I think she feels a little bit guilty. But if I had to say what she felt guilty *about*, it'd be a sort of multiple choice: moving, or not moving sooner; buying garage-sale furniture or not buying new furniture; buying new beds or not buying garage-sale beds; leaving Mrs. Hubbard or spending as much time as she did in Mrs. Hubbard's house.

Sam's helping her to cope. He's here a lot. Partly because of us and partly because—

I can see right now that this is never going to work. What I wanted to do was describe the whole apartment and our life in it, building up slowly like a wave gathering force until I got to *the* most important thing, but I can't stand it anymore and I have to say that *Sam Klemkoski's sculpture is in our apartment.*

That's right. In the corner of the living room. Just standing there in a majestic sort of way, so that all our hodgepodge furniture looks incredibly much better than it did in those garages where we found it.

Mom and I came over with a load of clothes the day before we moved in, and when we opened the door there it was, all finished and waxed smooth. And beautiful. It's not ours to keep, just on loan (the way things sometimes are in museums). Meanwhile, Sam says, it's to help my mother settle in.

There was something I'd been thinking about a lot, and one day when Sam was over and Mom wasn't home yet, I told him about it. It's that even if Jamie Ward was just my mother's good *friend* and Arthur Downie was really my *father*, either way, that made me half Australian, and what I wanted to do someday was to go to Australia.

"And so you should," said Sam, twiddling his toes. "Even though no one in this operation has any money to speak of. But who knows, Sydney. Maybe someday a rich merchant, who also happens to have exquisite taste and hands sensitive to the roll of the wood, will want to buy one of my sculptures. Or maybe we'll win the lottery. Or maybe you'll have to wait till you get to college and do a year as an exchange student and your mother and I'll come to visit you and we'll eat in all the Chinese restaurants in Sydney. Deal?"

"Deal." And when we shook on it, Sam's hand felt as rough as stone.

It was on the next-to-the-last day of school that Sam made his big announcement. "Since the point of the self-awareness journal was for you to *write* it and not for me to *read* it," he said, moving to the front of the room, "I am not going to ask you to hand your journals in."

"A-men," said Nat the Gat. "A-men," said Cissy and Mary Jo, Winkle, Brenda, Janet, and the others.

"A-men," I said, sighing deeply and closing my book.

"Not so fast there," said Sam, and for a minute I was afraid he had changed his mind. Instead, he said, "Take out a piece of paper for your last assignment. And listen carefully, because this is too long to put on the board, and when I've finished I want you to take it from there.

"It is years from now. You have accomplished a great deal, made many contributions to the world, and a leading New York publisher has asked you to write your autobiography. After you come back from mailing the final draft, you find page 242 on the floor of your den. What does that page say? If it's any help to you, there are 316 pages in the manuscript."

Page 242

It was snowing in New York that December day when my daughter and I came out of the restaurant after lunch and she had to hurry for the subway to get to her daughter's school before dismissal. I decided to walk along Fifth Avenue for a while, and just when I was ready to stop and catch a bus, I saw, up ahead, a huge bookstore with its window filled with copies of my most recent novel. I moved closer to the window and stood with my face pressed against it, wishing there was some way I could tell all those people hurrying by that it was mine. Then I noticed that one of the books was standing open to the dedication page, and I closed my eyes and whispered softly under my breath the words I'd used as a dedication in all my books:

"To Sam, who was there when it all began; to my mother, who believed in me; and, of course, to Wally, sans qui . . ." (Which is French and means, roughly, without whom it couldn't've been done.)

And of course the year couldn't end without Birdy-Morrison giving her "Goodbye, Girls" talk. She stood there in her morning-glory blue dress with her sagging bosoms, saying all the typical year-end things. I let my mind wander, thinking how, when what I'd written for Sam's final assignment really did come true and I was writing novels, I'd have to learn to end them: to have a climax and a denouement and not just let things fizzle out, the way they did in a self-awareness journal.

I mean, if this were a novel, something would have *happened* to Nat the Gat—either a debilitating but not serious illness or an elopement or maybe even being expelled—and not just that she was coming back to Hawthorne Hills next year, anyway, because her mother had decided it wasn't such a bad school, after all.

If this were a novel, I'd have a dog by now and be

planning an enormous party for the last day of school. Which I'm not.

My mother and Sam'd be married by now. Which they're not.

Jamie Ward would've invited me to spend the summer on his cattle station. Which he definitely hasn't.

And Sam Klemkoski would have found his rich merchant with exquisite taste who'd buy up all his sculptures so he'd never have to teach again. Which he hasn't.

All of which leads me to believe that "Plus ça change, plus c'est la même chose." (Or, as Natalie Gatling translated for us, "The more things change, the more they stay the same.")

"And now, girls"—Birdy-Morrison's voice had reached a crescendo—"let's all say a fond farewell to our own Sam Klemkoski, who is leaving us next year in order to teach at the Art Institute."

Everybody groaned, and the girls who'd hoped to be in Sam's class next year scuffed their feet against the floor.

"You knew, didn't you?" said Cissy, poking me in the ribs.

"You could've told us. So we could've gotten him a gift," said Mary Jo. "Maybe a tie, or a pair of socks."

I turned away from them, remembering how Sam had told me that if he was going to fall prey to the lure of the regular paycheck, he'd at least rather be in his own field.

I tuned back in just as Birdy-Morrison fairly shrieked, "Goodbye, girls. And happy summer."

Wally Martin was waiting for me after school. His parents (and Porter) had driven up to New Hampshire to get him, and they'd all gotten back late the night before.

"We could go somewhere," he said, as we walked down the hill and out onto the avenue.

"Yeah," I said, as we stood in line at the bus stop.

And for a minute I wondered what we were ever going to find to say to one another again. But by the time we were halfway downtown, he was telling me about his final exams and a book he'd read and a new record I just had to hear, and how Porter got carsick on the way home.

And by the time we got off at the end of the line, I'd told him about my summer job at the pizza place and how Sam wasn't coming back to Hawthorne Hills and how he planned to spend the summer fixing the central heating in his house. Which I took as a very good sign.

We rented a paddleboat at the harbor, climbed in, balancing ourselves, and paddled our way out into the middle. The sun was shining and there was a breeze, and I thought that what I would do when I got home was to start my summer journal. We talked, and we didn't talk. I trailed my hand in the water; and as I ran it along the underside of the boat I felt something sharp, and when I held my hand up, there was blood running down my finger.

"You okay?" asked Wally.

"Sure. It's nothing," I said.

"Boomerang blood," said Wally.

"Smoomerang blood," I said, as I held my finger up to the wind to dry.